RARE BIRDS

STORIES

L.S. JOHNSON

TRAVERSING Z PRESS

Traversing Z Press

San Leandro, California

www.traversingz.com

ISBN (paperback): 978-0-9988936-3-1

ISBN (ebook): 978-0-9988936-4-8

Library of Congress Control Number: 2019910168

Editing by Charlotte Ashley

Cover design by George Cotronis

Interior design and project management by Jennifer Uhlich

Printed in the United States of America

CONTENTS

RARE BIRDS

RARE BIRDS, 1959

1.

THERE WAS a point every evening when Elsa would look around and realize that the dinner rush was over, indeed had been over for some time. It always took her by surprise, even after months of working at the chophouse. Like everyone had sensed her exhaustion and up and went at the same time to give her some peace. She liked to think like that, liked to think that the customers were her friends, visitors in her large, wood-paneled living room, and she was just making sure they got a good square meal. It made it easier to deal with the jerks; it let her pretend that the large tip she got was for her kindness or her cooking and not because her uniform was too small. And when would Doug order her a new one, anyway?

She could ask Mary, Doug's wife, who sometimes helped with the hostessing; but Mary didn't like to be asked things. She left the day-to-day managing to

Doug, said she didn't have the head for it. Still, Elsa thought if she could just find the right moment, she could get Mary to do something. The skirt rode up when she bent down, and depending on the time of the month, the buttons would strain and gap. The last time Elsa had asked Doug he'd *yeah, yeah*ed her and added, *it's not doing you any harm, though.* And it wasn't; God knew she needed the tips. Her job was the difference between a good dinner for her husband and son and being on relief, and she had sworn never to go on relief again.

Still. As she cleared the table she looked at Mary out of the corner of her eye. All of the other waitresses were young and single, flirting with the cooks while the busboys flirted with them. She and Mary were older, and they both had little boys. If Mary were another waitress Elsa knew they'd be fast friends. Too, every now and then Mary would stand her a cup of coffee at the end of the night and they'd chat a little, mostly about their sons. Elsa looked forward to that more than she could say. To be herself again, even in her cheap uniform.

A little more time, she figured. A few more good chats and she could lean in close and say, *Mary, do a girl a favor, can't you get me a uniform that doesn't make me look like a sausage?*

As if in answer to her thoughts, a catalog suddenly appeared in front of her, and she felt a large, warm hand rest on the small of her back. *Uniform Supply*, the cover read, framed by a smiling waitress and chef. She turned to see Doug standing over her, his shadowed face unreadable.

"I can't let you take the catalog home," he said, "but if you stay after closing and pick out what you want, I'll order it first thing in the morning."

Elsa smiled as broadly as the waitress on the cover. It felt as if a huge weight had been lifted from her shoulders. "Of course I'll stay," she said.

She phoned Robert and told him she'd be late, and then settled into the stock room with a cup of coffee and the catalog, squinting at the pages in the dim light. The styles were line drawings so she couldn't quite tell which one matched the chophouse uniforms, and there were both half and whole sizes, and she couldn't find the sizing chart. She kept flipping and flipping … She heard Doug saying goodbye to the others, heard the shutters coming down.

Her last clear memory was of planning to tell Doug to forget it, that she couldn't make heads or tails of the thing. Everything afterwards came in flashes. Being held down across the boxes. Doug spitting words in her ear, dirty words no man had ever said to her before, and behind them a roaring noise like she was drowning. Choking on her sobs. He was so strong.

And when it was over, and she was fumbling with her clothes—Why didn't they go on right? Why couldn't she dress—when it was over, he told her in his normal voice that if she told anyone he would fire her, and she would never get work in another restaurant, and he would tell her husband and her son and everyone in the entire damn city just what a goddamn slut she was.

Her journey home was a blur; she felt almost insensible until she finally managed to close the apartment door. Only then did she begin shaking. She dared not enter their bedroom, she knew that Robert would know and what would happen then? Instead she dragged blankets onto the couch and buried herself inside them, pulling them over her head until she was cocooned in a hot darkness, shivering as if she was riddled with fever.

There she lay, all night, fighting back tears, terrified lest she make the slightest noise and wake her husband and son.

When she heard the alarm ringing, she made sure she was covered from head to toe, closed her eyes, and pretended to be asleep. The sounds of her son running around, Robert shushing him … it all made her feel sick and then ashamed of herself for feeling so about her family.

When Robert came into the living room to get his watch, she made herself limp and kept her breathing steady. But when he bent over her and touched her forehead, she cringed. He whispered, "Coming down with something? You feel pretty warm."

She nodded.

"Do you want me to phone the restaurant? I can call from the job site."

At once, panic filled her. "No," she croaked, her voice loud. "I'll call."

"Tell Doug you need a day off. It's the least he can do for keeping you so late." Robert laid his hand on her shoulder, caressing her through the blanket. "He better make it worth your while. I don't like you missing dinner. It's not good for Bobby, you know?"

As he spoke her mouth filled with bile. It was all she could do to nod again.

"Get some rest," he finally whispered, kissing her forehead.

There was the murmur of their voices, Bobby's distant *bye Mommy feel better* that she could not bring herself to acknowledge. She didn't want him to *see*, she didn't want either of them to see her. Only when she heard the door shut did she let herself start sobbing, waves of grief so violent as to choke her.

She was still crying when she managed to get herself to the bathroom and onto the toilet. The feel of the toilet paper made her feel sick and lightheaded. And then she smelled it, it was everywhere, and she tore off her clothing and climbed into the tub and opened the taps completely. She cried again, though she felt empty of all tears. At least in the water she couldn't smell herself, couldn't feel herself.

The phone rang out, echoing in the tiny apartment. The noise jarred her; she realized the water was up to her neck, rushing out of the overflow as fast as it poured in. She needed to do ... something, yet she could not think what, could only think that if she just stayed in the water nothing more could happen to her.

When the hot water turned cold she finally closed the taps. Her fingertips were shriveled. She could not look down at herself.

The sudden knocking felt like physical blows, making her mewl in fear.

"Elsa?" a female voice said.

Mary.

Elsa lurched out of the tub and seized her thin bathrobe, wrapping it tightly closed, then wrapped a towel over the robe until she felt cocooned.

Mary knocked again, three short raps and then a pause, followed by three more. Elsa started for the door only to hesitate. What if Mary knew, what if she had come to accuse her, even attack her? What had Doug said to her, what was he saying to everyone?

"Elsa," Mary said, "I know you're in there." She paused, as if weighing her words. "I know what he did," she said, her voice barely audible. "For God's sake, let me in."

Before Elsa knew what she was doing, she was across the living room, unlocking the door and flinging herself into Mary's arms.

The smell of frying eggs made her stomach knot, but she could not bring herself to speak. Mary moved around the kitchen with tight, efficient gestures that seemed to indicate either unease or a barely contained anger.

"I knew when you didn't show up this morning," she said as she slid the eggs onto a plate. "I knew then. Before——" The word came out so clipped she paused to swallow, then repeated, "——before, with the young ones, half of them would get on the next bus home, the other half would try and blackmail him." She put the plate in front of Elsa. "I honestly thought you were too old for him."

She stared at the plate——the eggs swimming in grease, the toast almost as yellow as the yolks——and tasted bile again.

"What did he tell you?" Mary asked.

She could not look up at Mary; she was terrified of what expression she might find. "That I'd never work again if I told anyone, and he'd tell Robert I'm a ..." Her throat closed around the word like a fist.

"Eat." Mary sat down across from her, folding her trembling hands one atop another. For the first time Elsa realized just how smooth Mary's hands were, how pristine her manicure, yet her engagement ring was as tiny as Elsa's own. She took up the fork and managed to get a piece of white between her lips. The scummy texture made her gag.

"I want to divorce him," Mary said in the same tight voice. "I can divorce him, if you'll sign a statement saying what he did."

Elsa looked up at her then and wished she hadn't. The grim face staring at her was terrifying. "A——a statement? Mary, I can't ... I haven't even told

Robert, I couldn't bear it if he knew. How could I face him—"

"I've looked into it before," Mary said, speaking over her. "I could do it by myself, but it would be costly, he would fight me tooth and nail. It's really mine, you see. Doug manages the restaurant and that's our income, but he started it with *my* money." She stared at her clenching hands. "The divorce is useless to me unless I can keep the restaurant, and he'll fight me for it. Unless I can show a judge what he really is." She met Elsa's gaze squarely. "I'll make it worth your while, don't you worry."

"But I can't tell Robert," Elsa said. She had started weeping again. "I couldn't last night ... and if I tell him now he'll ask himself, *why didn't she tell me when it happened?*" She looked beseechingly at Mary. "Please, I just want to forget. I don't care about the job, we'll get by. I just want to forget."

"Then Doug will say he fired you, and he'll spread it around that you propositioned him." Mary spoke the words flatly. "I know how he works, I've seen it before. I married an animal," she added under her breath. "A goddamn animal."

Elsa understood the words, understood what they meant, but still she couldn't quite believe it; it felt as if it was all happening to someone else. Finally, she asked, "Will I have to appear in court?"

"No. Just tell my lawyer what happened. Once you sign the papers you'll be done with it all."

"And the police? Won't they want ... evidence?"

Mary snorted. "Who said anything about the

police? There's no point in telling them anything. You washed away all the evidence." When Elsa began crying harder she took her hand, holding it as if she was unsure of what to do with it. "Look, Elsa. Even if you hadn't cleaned ... you know, we both know that wouldn't have been enough. They'd have wanted to see bruises, ripped clothes; they'd want witnesses who heard you hollering for your life. You know it, I know it, and God help us, Doug knows it."

Elsa stared down at the shimmering white and yellow on her plate. "I don't know," she whispered. "I don't know."

"I'll tell you what I know: what I'm offering you is the only thing that will get you out of this without putting your family on skid row." She suddenly squeezed Elsa's hand, so hard Elsa yelped in pain. "You can't survive without two salaries. I can see it just by looking at this place. I'll pay you what you were getting, and you won't even have to work for it. You just have to help me get rid of him."

Elsa's fingers were starting to go numb. Only then did she notice on the back of Mary's tightly gripping hand was a spray of fine, red bumps like pimples, each with a tiny black center. Where had they come from?

"What about your little boy?" she whispered.

Mary's grip increased. "Better he grow up without a father, than be raised by the likes of him."

The taste of egg in Elsa's mouth was like something rotting. She couldn't think on what to say or do, she could only sit there, her eyes endlessly leaking and her hand tingling and throbbing. At last she nodded and sighed with relief when Mary let go. She brought her sore hand to her chest, massaging it to bring the blood back to her fingertips.

And then she held out her hand between them, staring as a rash of red dots broke out across her knuckles.

She stayed home sick for three days.

On the fourth day Elsa told Robert she was going to the doctor, but instead of going to their family doctor she went to a specialist. There she handed over her small savings and took off her blouse, showing him the bumps everywhere: patches on her back, on her arms, all with different shades of brown at their centers.

She did not tell him how she opened one with a straight pin and teased forth a tiny brown feather, wet with a clear liquid, spreading its miniscule barbules as it emerged into the light of the bathroom.

The specialist gave her a cream that cost her the grocery money in her pocketbook, suggested she change her laundry detergent, and sent her on her way.

On the fifth day Elsa told Robert she was going back to work, but instead she put on her best day dress and dark stockings and a long-sleeved jacket and gloves and went to the heart of the city, where she met Mary at her lawyer's office. There, she told what had happened in a small, sobbing voice, ashamed to raise her eyes despite the lawyer's gentle tone and the hand he laid over hers. While they typed it up properly she drank a very strong cup of coffee and wondered why everything felt so wrong: why she didn't feel better for telling, why Mary still looked so grim, why everyone else looked so pleased at hearing what had happened.

When the typist brought in the clean copy she reached for a pen to sign it, only to be stopped by Mary, who touched Elsa's gloved hand with her own. "You're sure it's enough?" she asked the lawyer. "To get *everything*? I want to break him, not just divorce him."

"Mrs. Phillips," the lawyer said with that pleased smile on his face, "with all your evidence, and now this? You're going to clean him out. He'll be lucky to leave the courtroom with the shirt on his back."

Slowly Elsa picked up the pen and signed. Beside her Mary exhaled, as if releasing something that she had long held inside. At once, though, her sigh became a hacking cough. She hunched over in her chair, coughing and spluttering, waving away the lawyer's offer of water; Elsa leaned over her and pressed a handkerchief into her hand.

"Thank you," Mary muttered. She stayed hunched over, coughing into the handkerchief and dabbing at her eyes and face. At last she sat up and tucked the handkerchief into her purse, so only Elsa saw the black feather gummed to the cloth.

2.

Elsa slid the raw eggs into the pan, careful not to break the yolks. Bobby liked his eggs just so, he liked to eat all the white right up to the edges of the yellow circle, then cut a single small opening in which to dip his toast. He was like his father in this: the precision with his habits, wanting everything to be just right.

Elsa knew she was no longer just right; she was becoming less right with every passing week. Neither the doctor's prescription nor her own lotions had done anything to stop the rash that now covered her from head to foot. She had tried vitamins, powders, baths with salts and baths with oils; still the bumps spread and swelled, some with white heads now, some with nearly black ones as well as brown. Her family believed she must have eaten something poisonous, she would have to be patient and let it work its way through her. When they said this Elsa had thought *Mary*, but kept her mouth shut.

Had Elsa's mother still been alive she might have said something different. Her mother had often told her bedtime stories that weren't in books, stories from *the old world*, stories her mother's mother had told, and her mother before that, and so on ... Stories of women who were changed into things, river rocks and fleet deer, nightingales and sparrows and tall, twisting trees. Always they were betrayed in some fashion and then swiftly changed, to save them from a worse fate. *And then she was no more of this world,* her mother would always finish, and then she would pretend to show Elsa something from the woman in question—a leaf, a feather. But such endings had never felt like escapes to Elsa. They felt like condemnations, and her dreams would be filled with monstrous images of animals with women's faces, their silent mouths screaming endlessly.

Only now did Elsa understand her child-self had been right, that those stories weren't fantasies. They were *warnings*.

She wasn't escaping anything; she was being imprisoned in her own body. The bumps kept spreading, and her joints ached. Her fingers and toes curled when she rested, and her elbows were becoming stiff. What would happen if she became too sick, too strange-looking, to go outside? Who would help her, who would care for her?

She knew in her heart it would not be Robert, and she would not so burden her son.

As she arranged his food on the plate she looked at Bobby's bowed head, and beside him her stony-gazed husband, still staring at the front of the newspaper like it was the world. Mary's lawyer had called to discuss her statement—Elsa hadn't expected anyone to call her, she had thought once she signed the paper it was over—and Robert had taken the call. His first rush of anger had been horrible but also a relief, she had spent so long anticipating it; what she had not anticipated was that he already believed her to have been unfaithful with Doug, and the statement merely confirmed what he had *heard*.

So much said in the days and nights since, that could not be unsaid.

She could only think of two people who might have told him such a thing, and only one who could have done so without getting punched.

She put the eggs before Bobby, kissed his head, and hurried back into the kitchen. The smell of her son in her nostrils. Robert slept on the sofa now, and only responded when she told him basic things: what was for dinner, who had phoned during the day. All the money was in his name, and if he started talking to a lawyer——? Only now did she see that her statement might work against her just as it had worked against Doug.

Even if she could afford a lawyer of her own it would get ugly quick, and she would have to relive it all. And Bobby … to put him through all that, what would it do to him?

Could she bear to let her son go?

She began washing the pan, watching her reddened hands in the water as she scrubbed, her knuckles flexing white with the effort—

—and then stared, open-mouthed, at the line of erupting bumps along her hand and forearm. Small brown tubes jutted out from her irritated skin, their tufted ends waving like tiny ferns in the water. She raised her hands, turning them one way and another, and then ran a soapy finger along the lines of feathers, marveling at their plastic feel, at how the tufts were already drying and softening.

Only then did the enormity of it hit her. She

pulled at a feather, trying to remove it, but the pain was swift and shocking: it was *in* her, it was part of her. Still she raised her hand to her mouth and bit down hard on the shaft, wrenching and pulling until at last it came free. At once the wound began to bleed, not the bleeding of a normal scratch or scrape but freely, copiously bleeding, splattering red across the countertops and sink, dyeing the dishwater pink as she fumbled for a clean towel and pressed it to the wound.

Elsa bent low over the sink then, swallowing her sobs so Robert and Bobby would not hear, for she understood, at last, how everything she had ever imagined about her life to come had been lost the moment the first bump appeared.

She had expected another apartment like her own, a tiny, cramped space among dozens like it, but as she made her way to Mary's address it was as if she had crossed into another world. Here were large, sprawling Tudor cottages, with actual lawns and pruned shrubbery; here were flowers, spilling from pots and twining their way around railings. Elsa had never known the neighborhood existed. Even the city noise seemed muffled, as if she had passed through some kind of bubble to reach this place.

She found the house and was again surprised: it was one of the largest, with gabled windows and a quaint little turret. It was something that belonged in a wealthy suburb, not here.

It was all my money. How much money did Mary actually have? Until now Elsa had been debating her approach, because she hadn't believed, couldn't believe, that Mary would utter such a lie, and to Robert no less. But this storybook house, the pristine lawn and the lace curtains and the driveway, that she actually had a car—oh, it made something grow hot and tight in Elsa's stomach, made her hands into fists so that she had to punch the doorbell with a reddened knuckle.

When the door swung open she pushed her way in before Mary could protest, storming into the silent, pristine living room and rounding on her. "What did you say to Robert?"

Mary shut the door and locked it.

"He's filing for divorce, Mary. He's filing for *sole custody.*" She was trembling with anger. "You said nothing would happen. No trials, no police, just make a statement. You got what you wanted. Why did you *do* this?"

Mary looked at her levelly, then angled her head. "Drink?"

"Damn you, answer me," Elsa ground out. Her own tears were blinding her; she wiped at her eyes with the back of her hand, only to yelp as the tip of a feather poked her.

"Well, I'm going to have one." Mary went to the little cart in the living room; in the silence there was only the sound of Elsa's shuddering breath and ice clinking against glass. At last Mary said, "I didn't intend to say anything to Robert. He came up to me in the playground the other day, my son was standing right there. What was I supposed to say in front of him?" She downed two fingers of Scotch and poured another. "They've been teasing him at school, saying things about Doug … so I thought, there's no reason for him to know the truth about his father, not now. So, I told him and a few of the other mothers … I said it was an affair, I just meant to soften it a little. And then all of a sudden Robert was there, I mean he came to my son's *school* for God's sake, and all those snoops were listening to us, waiting to catch me out." She suddenly rounded on Elsa. "What would you have me say?" she yelled.

"The truth," Elsa yelled back. "The goddamn truth! What about *my* boy? Robert's taking him away, Mary, he says I can't be trusted!"

Mary took another long sip. "You know," she said in a normal tone of voice, "I think I did you a favor."

The words brought Elsa up short. "What?"

"You heard me. I did you a favor." She took a step closer to Elsa, her eyes narrowing. "I think you didn't want to tell him because you knew, deep down, that he would never believe you. What kind of husband believes a stranger over the woman he supposedly loves? What kind of husband lets the mother of his son go to work each day looking like a slut?" She finished the second drink and wiped her mouth on her sleeve. "And then he comes to me—to *me*—asking if there was any funny business between you and Doug? In *public*? In front of my *son*? I don't think he gives a damn about you. I think you're just a thing to him, like a car, and you're just not running right anymore."

With a cry Elsa flung herself forward, hitting Mary as hard as she could; they tumbled onto the carpet. She pushed herself up to sitting and brought her fist down, once and again, trying to beat away the smirk on Mary's face.

On the third blow, there was a cracking noise; Elsa froze, her hand raised. Behind the blood and the bruising weal on Mary's nose was something else, something black and shell-like. She looked at the hint of beak, then at the blood on her own spotted knuckles, and sat back with a whimper.

"Maybe we deserve this," she whispered. "Maybe it's a curse, we brought it on ourselves, all this deceit and ugliness …" Her eyes were running, running. "God, why didn't I just tell him that night …"

"Because he's a man," Mary said, her voice garbled; she rolled her head to the side and spat blood, then propped herself up on her elbows. "Because you know that no matter how you explained it, he'd never touch you again. Not after *that*." She made a cutting gesture with her hand. "We're changing because of men, Elsa. All the gods are men. All the doctors are men. All the cops and the judges and the shrinks are men. If Doug had done that to a man they would have hung him from the nearest lamppost; if a man suddenly started spouting feathers they'd have a cure within a year or worship him like he was the goddamn Second Coming. Us? Oh, we're hysterical, we're crazy, we can't be trusted … and

when we try to say *no*, this is what we get." She staggered to her feet, touching her nose gingerly. "If you
ask me, this is just an allergic reaction to all the men
in our lives."

The furious outpouring made Elsa cringe, but not
as much as it would have, once. "You shouldn't speak
like that," she said to the carpet. "You should think of
your boy—"

"My son hates me," Mary said flatly. "Thinks I
drove his daddy away." She tapped the black spot with
her fingernail, wincing at the clicking sound. "He told
me the other night either I let him live with Doug or
he's going to leave the day he turns eighteen and
never see me again. He's started getting into fights at
school … now I have to decide whether I want to
raise a delinquent, or let Doug raise a monster."

She went over to the cart and poured two more
Scotches; when she held one out Elsa got to her feet
and took it. The amber liquid burned her throat.
Robert never let her have liquor …

But Robert wasn't around anymore. Robert would
probably never be around again.

"You always think you're different," Mary said,
her back to her Elsa. "You get married and you see
other women's husbands and you think, *not me, my guy
won't ever go around chasing skirt like that.* You have a son
and you think, *not my boy, he'll never go bad, he'll never be
disrespectful or cruel like those other kids.*" She looked at
Elsa and her eyes were red. "My son is going to leave
me all alone like this!"

She shoved her sleeve up to her elbow, revealing

lines of molting feathers, small and fine like new blades of grass.

Elsa stared at her. "And what happens to him if he stays? How will you take him to school, looking like that? The doctor? A baseball game? Maybe it's not a choice between a delinquent or a monster. Maybe it's a choice between some kind of normal or, or whatever *this* is."

She raised her hand to point at Mary's face, but found she could not straighten her finger completely; the knuckle simply would not yield. Her crooked hand hung in midair, spotted with down, and Elsa understood then she was speaking not to Mary but to herself, that a door was closing in her own heart.

When she returned home the apartment was dim and quiet. There were a last few boxes of Robert's things by the door; the bedroom suddenly seemed large without Bobby's narrow cot against the wall. The silence pressed in on her, it made her skin crawl, and with a racing heart she hurried into the living room and turned on the radio. The familiar orchestration, the first crooning words, they all soothed her:

And now the purple dusk of twilight time
Steals across the meadows of my heart

She moved around the room, turning on lamps, smoothing down her hair as she prised off her hat and coat. Her whole body was tense; she realized she was listening for footsteps in the hall because she hadn't made any dinner, and what would Robert say if he came home and there was no dinner waiting?

But she didn't need to worry about that anymore.

Love is now the stardust of yesterday
The music of the years gone by

As she went to hang up her things in the bedroom she paused before the dresser mirror, staring at herself. Her face was mottled with bumps like she was a teenager again, but even more frightening were her eyes: they were veined with black, as if a pen were bleeding into the whites. Her eyesight was fine— better than fine lately, the world had taken on a purplish tint that seemed to yield a new sharpness. Now as she gazed at herself she realized that she could actually see it, she could see the black feathering outwards, it was filling her eyes—

She clapped her hands over her face like a child and when she looked again it was still there, though now her reflection swam from her tears.

But that was long ago
Now my consolation
Is in the stardust of a song

Elsa stood in the little bedroom and cried, her coat and hat slipping to the floor. She cried for herself, for Mary; she cried for her son and the lies she had told him to ease their parting; she cried for her empty room and her empty arms and her body that was leaving her, for her own fear and loneliness, for all the women who had ever been hurt so, for all the women made birds.

3.

The knocking, loud and sudden, made Elsa squawk with fright. It took a moment to calm her fluttering heart and turn down the television, a complicated process of hooking the dial with her fingernail and nudging it. She had always been proud of her hands, how small and shapely they were, but they were nearly gone now. Her fingers had first become painfully stiff, then fused into three clawlike digits. Now calluses were growing over what had been her finger joints, just before the first line of feathers.

She waddled to the door, trembling with both nerves and hope. It was the wrong day for her grocery delivery, and rent wasn't due for a week yet. She had told herself she was staying in the apartment because it was familiar and she did not want to burden her few, distant relatives; but in truth it was because leaving felt too final to bear. What if Robert decided to come back, or Bobby came looking for her? What if Mary, with all her money, was able to find a cure, only couldn't find Elsa to share it with her?

But when Elsa looked through the peephole, there was nothing.

She turned off the overhead light, then seized the

chain with her beak and tested it, making sure it was securely fastened; only then did she open the door a crack.

Before her, on the ratty welcome mat, was a paper grocery bag with a note clipped to one side. Elsa couldn't see inside the bag, but she could smell it: meat and spices and something that she had only recently learned to identify.

Seeds.

Crouching low, she eased one clawed hand through the gap, hooking the bag and pulling it to the door. The note wasn't a note but a postcard, a picture topped with fancy calligraphy: *Philomela and Procne*. The light in the hallway was dim, but in the last few weeks Elsa's eyesight had become nothing short of remarkable, the world taking on a purple-tinted sharpness that let her see even the gnats that made their way through her window screens. Now she tilted the postcard to see the whole image, only to cry out.

Two women with the heads of birds, their spread arms sprouting wings.

"My Nana was like you," a voice said from the left.

Elsa jerked backwards, terrified; she tried to shove the door closed but it caught on the bag.

"I'm sorry! I didn't mean to frighten you. I'm Doreen, I live downstairs." A housedress and apron suddenly appeared, filling the gap between door and frame. "I—I saw you the other night," she continued, dropping to a conspiratorial whisper. "Taking out your trash. My Nana went the same way, and I just thought …"

She trailed off; Elsa could see her hands wringing atop her apron. Slowly she rose to standing, taking in Doreen's wide-eyed face, the flush in her cheeks.

"My momma used to make that meatloaf for Nana, she always liked it." Her blush deepened. "And I thought … my husband's away for a few days, and you don't seem to have anyone who can do for you."

Still Elsa just looked at her, her breath coming in whistling gasps through her beak. As frightened as she was, she could not stop staring at Doreen: there was a strange mottling on her arm and jawline, some kind of discoloration.

Elsa could think of very few things that would mark a woman in just those places.

"Well," Doreen said, ducking her head. "I'm, ah, I'm downstairs in 2B, if you ever need—"

"Wait," Elsa said quickly.

That is, she meant to say *wait*, but it came out as another squawk; still Doreen paused as Elsa worked the chain off and opened the door completely. Only then did she realize she was letting this woman see her, really see her, when she could barely look at herself and dared not go out save in the dead of night.

But Doreen just smiled. "You look like her," she said. She reached out and stroked Elsa's shoulder, and the sensation made Elsa's eyes well, made the purple world shimmer for a moment.

"Coffee?" Elsa asked, and this time she didn't wince at the sound of her own voice.

"Really?" Doreen's smile grew warm, open. "I'd like that."

She bent over, picking up the bag, and Elsa saw it then: how she flinched at some pain in her arm, how for a moment her skin rippled with the first hint of a rash that just as quickly faded. For now, but what might happen when next he struck her, or abused her in some other way?

There could not be so much hurt in the world, Elsa could not believe it; yet she could *see* it in this woman, like something sleeping.

But if she could see it, maybe she could stop it.

She stepped aside and let Doreen in.

MARIGOLDS

PARIS, 1775

1.

THIS ROOM IS THE UNIVERSE. This bed the earth, the ceiling the sky. Somewhere in the plaster heavens above me are the clear brushstrokes that will flare like sunlight when I will them into being.

When *I* will them.

I watch Maurepas enter the room, framed by my knees. He is plump and old, like the others that come to us, ministers and directors, princes and counts. Smelling of cognac and roasted birdflesh, their doughy skin scored by silks and velvets cut for younger bodies. He strips now, this minister, and when the last piece of cloth is discarded he is just another old man.

All their power is stolen, Mémé says. *Even that of kings: they steal their power, and as such it can be stolen back. Why should they have so much and we so little? Do we not come into the world the same, and leave it the same? What does anyone truly possess, save the body she is born with?*

Our bodies and their power, the only true power in the world.

Or so Mémé says, and we are supposed to believe.

Maurepas watches the blood between my legs. Already his lips have parted, his face become damp with sweat; the air between us crackles. Is it already beginning? Do they all yield so easily? These men who rule France, rule it with pen and paper and sword and shot, all paying in coin and dissipation to taste me.

Mémé teaches us that the spasms we feel are not pain; they are *hunger*. Every wrenching ache is not some ancient curse; it is *anticipation*. Our bodies are doing what they were made to do: open completely, the better to impose our will upon the universe.

I feel his energy flow into me, stoking my own fire. His mouth between my legs, tasting me before he rises over me, his lips wet. I close my eyes; I cannot bear to look at him. *It smells like marigolds*, they tell each other in the salon, smirking like naughty boys. Thinking they are taking from us, gaining a few extra years, a last rally of youth. When instead it is we who take from them, we take their power and their vigor, we take and we take and we take—

Somewhere inside me I am crying out *Isabella*—

I open my eyes and set the swirling heavens alight in a glorious golden rush.

We are remaking the world.

Or so Mémé says, and we are supposed to believe.

As Maurepas leaves he kisses me, his mouth sloppy and redolent. "I feel alive again," he whispers in my ear. "Like I am twenty years younger. Marvelous, Claire, simply marvelous …"

I hate this time, after, when he is once more just a debauched minister and I his whore. Yet I cannot bring myself to tell him the truth: he has gained nothing. If anything, he looks older, older and tired. How can they delude themselves, that a taste of my blood is the elixir they crave? Do they honestly believe they are the first to try, that no one has dared to taste a woman's courses before?

Or perhaps this too is part of what we create, when we make the symbol appear on our ceilings: this irrational belief in their own renewal.

I wash my face and my mouth, wash between my legs, and bind myself in fresh linen. Only when I feel clean do I creep, barefoot, into the hall. The air is hot and thick and everywhere I hear sighs, panting cries, the grunting of the men. I was lucky tonight: Maurepas is a quick one. Some of the others will be at it till dawn.

A quick one, and I was already on the brink before he arrived, as we are told to be. *You must feel pleasure, real pleasure, or it will not happen,* Mémé had said. *I make them wait before going to you, so as to give you time. Bring yourself as close to the moment as possible.* From a box she had pulled out objects, feathers and patches of soft fur and ivory carved to look like a man's organ, all while I blushed and squirmed. *Imagine you are with a lover, or would you prefer one of these? You can try anything you fancy. Or is there something else you like? Louisa, peasant girl that she was, used to use marrows, and Aimée has a little embroidered pillow, very firm ...*

But I have no need of toys, or imaginary lovers. All I need is to envision the door across from mine, and what lies behind it, and what might happen should it one day open for me.

Isabella's door.

I crouch before it now, humble with longing. I know every inch of its surface, every whorl of the grain. The key is always in her lock so I can only listen. The space between door and floor glows brightly. Turgot likes to see her and I cannot blame him. Were it myself, I would fill her room with candles, to see every inch of her—

She mewls like a kitten, gasping and crying theatrically, and I grin at the parquet. Poor old baron. He probably thinks himself a great lover. He is always preening when he leaves.

But then her noises change.

I press my ear to the door. My hand drifts between my legs yet again; every sound of flesh against flesh leaves me breathless. I can even *smell* her, not marigolds but something sweet and tangy and peppered all at once, like the rush of air on a spring morning, everything blooming and blossoming—

When at last she cries out I shudder in turn. A moment later Turgot makes a barking cry that trails off into a pathetic bout of coughing.

Isabella.

When her door finally opens I am back in my

room, watching through the keyhole as the fat ass laps at her neck, then gropes between her legs one last time. Shoving his red-tipped fingers in his mouth all at once, like a child.

Isabella watches him go—and then she looks at my door. Does she know I'm watching? Is she truly looking, or is she merely lost in blissful recollections of the Baron de Laune's gouty mass?

I dare not move. I cannot even breathe until she closes her door once more. The hall silent and dark now. Lifeless.

What does Isabella imagine, while she waits for Turgot to arrive?

2.

"… Maurepas," Mémé recites, sliding her finger down the page of the ledger spread open on her lap. So many names and only eight of us. Have there really been so many? "Sartine. Vergennes. Diderot. Forbonnais. Malesherbes. Albert." She smiles down at the page. "And of course, Turgot …"

We all look at Isabella, who blushes. She is Turgot's favorite, which makes her Mémé's favorite. Bread at more than three *sous* a pound, the prices driving people to protest—you can see the joy in Mémé's gaunt little face when Turgot arrives. The tangible result of all our perverse couplings. He comes now in a plain carriage, to avoid the crowds that each month are becoming a little more violent, a little less reasonable.

Not that reason ever had a place in this.

Mémé counts out our money, each coin washed clean. It's more than any other brothel in Paris, even the finer ones. But I barely glance at the coins in my hand; I no longer study Mémé's odd ageless face, her hands at once lined and strong; I no longer wonder at the strange circular scoring on her floor, how every room is arranged so the beds point west. All I can think on is her desk, where she draws the symbols and hands them over one by one, almost careless in her gestures. Nothing more than circles and lines and curves, the whole twisted so as to seem a knot; yet each time it is a different symbol, never quite the same. Each time, too, we must paint it on another's ceiling. We never see what is on our own.

Isabella balancing on my bed that first night, frowning at the slip of paper in her hand, the brush in her other dripping that queer cloudy liquid, and the straining arch of her bare leg—

Somehow the symbols and our blood make things happen. Sometimes Mémé has us paint them even when we are not bleeding, but in the moment they merely brighten a little, there is no blinding flash. *Without our blood, all we can do is nudge matters along*, she explained. *But when our blood comes: that is our time. Our ancestors knew this. They secluded their women when the moon waxed, lest they inadvertently ruin the crops, or kill a man through lovemaking. Only I learned to control our power through the sigils. With a clear sigil before us, a powerful man to take from, and our blood flowing? That is when we can lay our hands upon the tiller of the world and change its course for good.*

Save that I no longer want to go where Mémé says, if ever I did. I no longer care about Paris, or bread, or power. The only world I want to make is one where Isabella holds out her hand to me as she did the first day I saw her, except this time she doesn't let go, she instead draws me close and presses her lips to mine—

All I need is the right symbol, the right *sigil* as Mémé says, only I do not know how to make them.

Not yet.

Our week may be done, but we cannot relax. We still have the rest of the month to survive. There is our own bread to earn, the shopping to do. We change the lantern outside from red glass to clear and we dress plainly to run our errands, our hair tucked into mobcaps and worn muslin aprons over our skirts.

We go out in the world and see what we have wrought.

We go in threes, three and three and then a pair with Mémé. She takes whoever she feels needs encouragement, the better to exhort them at length. *This is not for our own gain, this is for everyone, for France herself. I have seen them at their estates. I have watched them dance and screw, drunk on their own gluttony, while children die of starvation at their gates. It is not right, it is not right. But we have the power to change this—the power and the understanding.*

Today, however, there is no Mémé and her philosophizing; today there is only Isabella at my side. Aimée too, but she stops to peer in every shop window, she dawdles and hurries after us and dawdles again. She has kept her little *mouche* on, the red drop below her lip that we all wear during that week, the mark of our specialty. She only tossed her head at Isabella's tut-tutting. Men eye her as they pass—after so many months word is getting around—they eye her and she simpers and flirts, loving the attention.

I try my best to ignore her, to imagine that it is only Isabella and me. Our list in her careful print: soap, pigeons for our supper, more cognac for the gentlemen. Her arm in mine, her laughter sweet in my ear. Would that it could last forever.

Aimée draws close to us, peering over Isabella's shoulder and giggling. "Does your wild girl even know what cognac is?"

"Aimée," Isabella scolds, but says nothing more.

But it is true: I was a wild thing when Isabella found me. Digging through the garbage at the waterfront for anything I might eat or barter, begging in the Marais, hand to mouth and day to day, unable to think on anything save making it through one more night …

Your wild girl. Wild with despair, wild with hope at the sight of Isabella's beckoning hand. Her hair perfectly curled and pinned and powdered, her dress so creamy and bright it seemed to glow against the filth of the street. The shimmer of her décolletage, her lips rouged scarlet, and just beneath that single red drop.

I took her hand and I looked into her brown eyes and I thought, *I will follow you anywhere*.

And then I realized: I was making a *choice*. For the first time in my life I was *choosing* my fate.

No one else could have brought me to this. No one else could make me part my legs for these men.

As soon as Isabella took my hand, I would have followed her to hell.

Our own neighborhood is as peaceful as on any day, but as we draw near the market the mood turns ugly. Everywhere voices are thick with discontent. Hats are pulled low, hands raised over mouths as people mutter to each other. There is even an outright duel in an alley, despite the laws: swords flashing, the young men furious as they lunge at each other, scrabbling for purchase on the slop-covered cobblestones. Barefoot, lean children run past us, tormenting a mangy cat. Half-lidded eyes running over us. The very air making my stomach churn.

I clutch at Isabella's arm, pressing close to her. "Never fear," she says. "They cannot harm us."

But she is only parroting what Mémé tells us, that our safety is part of the sigils. *You enact not only the great change but your place in it as well.* Yet who decides what our place is, other than Mémé? Who knows what she really puts in her drawings, what retribution they might invoke?

My only hope is that she would protect Isabella, for Isabella has Turgot.

The market, at least, is its usual chaotic maze of long, low tables overflowing with wares: vegetables, meats, raw fish stinking atop the shredded pages of gazettes; scraps of fabrics and old clothes that the young women crowd around, hoping for some pricey bit of lace; pots and pans and tools, rusted but service-able or new and gleaming. I can sense, behind us, Aimée's head darting from side to side. This is where Mémé found her, a clerk's daughter trying to make herself appear something more. She had lost her virtue to a butcher's agent and was desperate for a man with clean hands. Her last customer was Malesherbes, which means she has not come far at all.

As we move deeper into the market the sunlight disappears. I look up, thinking perhaps a storm is coming, but it is only the shadow of the pillory. Three bodies are silhouetted within, slumped in their stocks. The stone front of the tower is smeared with rotting foodstuffs and a man offers us some bruised fruits: would us ladies like to throw one?

Aimée reaches for his basket but Isabella grabs her arm. "Leave them be," she says, her voice low.

"It's just a bit of fun—"

"Leave them be," Isabella repeats, and for the first time I hear anger in her voice. "There but for the grace of God, Aimée."

"As if we're like them," Aimée says, her cheeks

flushing. "Soon enough it will be your precious Turgot up there, or hanging from—"

Isabella shakes her hard, cutting her off. "For God's sake," she hisses. "What if someone hears? There are spies everywhere, you'll get us all arrested."

"Not you," Aimée retorts. "Never her precious Isabella. Take care," she adds to me, "this one will do anything Mémé asks, even if it means ratting on you."

At her words, Isabella recoils, as if Aimée had struck her. "I would never," she says, a tremor in her voice. "I would *never*." She looks at me and I see her eyes are full. Before I can speak, she looks away again. "Forget the vegetables," she says to the ground. "Let's just go back."

But I cannot move. The tremulous *never*. The anger in her voice, her anger and her *tears*. Always, she had seemed to believe wholeheartedly in Mémé's scheme—

"Isabella," I say. A dozen half-formed phrases tangling in my mind.

At the far end of the market, a group of men suddenly appear, causing a murmur to run through the crowd. Conversations die away as everyone turns. Each man is spattered with powder—

No, not powder. *Flour.*

"Fifteen sous a loaf!"

The roar comes from somewhere in their group. It is picked up at once, the call echoing through the market, deep and furious.

Isabella grabs my hand.

Fifteen sous!

At once the space around us fills with bodies, male and female, old and young, pressing against us. They wave spoons and knives, sticks and hammers.

Fifteen sous!

We are being pushed forward, carried along in the crowd. Behind us, Aimée whispers, "What should we —" But Isabella hushes her, a single hiss, her hand rigid around mine.

An older man climbs onto one of the tables, calling out for us to stop. Another climbs beside him and with a polite smile punches him in the head, knocking him into the crowd that swarms over him without a glance.

Isabella twists beside me. A hand is pulling at her skirts, she pushes it away. Another chuckle, somewhere in back—

And then Aimée is gone.

I start to turn, to go after her, but Isabella pulls me close. Hands are groping me, I cannot tell who is touching me. My foot catches on a body, a woman huddled on the ground, covering her child as the mob trample thoughtlessly over her.

The mob swells, pushing towards the rue de la Petite Truanderie. We keep our arms wrapped around each other. Isabella is stepping to the left at every opportunity and I do the same. Throughout, she keeps her head raised, keeps looking ahead, and I do the same.

I will follow you anywhere.

We round the corner, still side-stepping left. We are nearly at the edge of the crowd now. Above the rumbling of voices, I hear a high-pitched shrieking and I think *Aimée!* But I see now it is a horse at the intersection; the people have rolled the carriage and they are swarming over it with sticks and clubs and both horse and driver are screaming for mercy beneath the blows. Fruit tumbles from the cart, crushed into the ground by the unseeing feet of the mob. Just a farmer and his animal, and what in God's name do they have to do with the price of bread?

What is Mémé creating, that would make people act so?

I look at Isabella and her eyes are red, her lips trembling; still she keeps her head up, keeps wiggling free of the pawing hands, keeps moving to the left as best she can.

At last the mob halts before a building. The people press together, some rising on tiptoe to see what is happening. They are looting a bakery, flinging loaves through the smashed windows, passing sacks of flour out hand over hand only to see them torn apart, releasing white clouds into the air, turning the looters to ghosts.

"I cannot help it! I don't decide the prices!" the baker bellows from the floor above, his voice echoing in the street. "Go attack Turgot, go to Versailles, they are selling the very grain from our fields to line their own pockets!"

The mob roars back, a bestial sound. Isabella seizes the corner of a building, dragging us bodily forward. Across the street is the rue Mondétour and a hint of open space around the bend—

And then I smell the fire.

The flames fill the ground-floor windows, licking up the walls, smoke billowing into the street. A woman screams from somewhere within, screams and screams, and a ripple of mocking laughter runs through the crowd. Now they begin throwing things back into the bakery: rags, trash, whatever is to hand and might burn.

A little boy appears above the heads, balancing on a man's shoulder, and begins to sing:

> *Panis angelicus*
> *fit panis hominum*
> *Dat panis coelicus*
> *figuris terminum*
> *O res mirabilis*
> *Manducat Dominum*
> *Pauper, servus et humilis*

And just then, listening to his sweet soprano and the screams of the people dying—just for a moment, the world flashes terrifyingly golden.

It is *happening*.

Isabella pulls me across the street and around the bend, so fast I nearly lose my pattens as we hurry back to the safety of the brothel.

"Creation," Mémé tells us that night, "is always violent: look at how babies come into the world, how plants rip their seed-shells apart, how birds hack and bite their way free of the egg. Is it no wonder that the mobs tear apart the bakeries, that they burn houses regardless of who might be within? They, too, are trying to wrest power from those who have it. They simply don't know a better way."

And what might they do to us, I want to ask, *if they knew you thought fit to starve them for your own schemes, using perversion and witchcraft?*

Outside there is still so much noise. Scattered cheers and shouts, the spatter of pistol shots—there were militia on the streets, Louisa reported breathlessly, there was talk of adding gibbets to the Place de Grève.

Aimée's room is dark and silent. I can still hear the screaming, can still smell the fire in my hair.

What have we done?

3.

It is nearly our week again when Mémé finally goes out. To look for custom, or so she says. She goes to the Opéra and the Comédie, salons and supper-parties, with blood-red mouth and crimson gown and one of us in tow: a sample. She lets the men boast about their connections, their power, their proximity to the king's ear—and when she thinks she has found a suitable candidate she takes him to a room or her coach, the better to be fawned over.

And you know who does all the work, Aimée had confided in me, *while she gets away with a few kisses.*

Aimée …

I wait until the brothel is quiet, save for a trio of young noblemen who came to the door with a fat purse and a great deal of wine. We drew lots for them, the other girls salivating at the money, and I pretended to be disappointed, but wasn't it a sign? Their loud voices cover my noises as I tiptoe into Mémé's room and go to her little desk.

The drawers are locked. And if I try to break them open, and am caught …

I search the rest of her room, looking for a key, trying to think on what to do. Love letters at her bedside, from men—perhaps she has done a little more than kissing. At first her bookshelves seem mostly libertine novels, but when I open one up a pamphlet falls out, a tract on grain. More pamphlets and broadsheets are wedged between the books, many of their authors' names familiar.

There is nothing, however, to explain the sigils.

And then I open her commode.

It is filled with shreds of paper, smelling of urine, but I can see the marks clear enough. Letters, stretched and cramped, twisted and combined.

The sigils are words, their letters layered over each other to form one shape.

I can make out a few of them, words like *King* and *People*. Numbers too: *60 livres*—that is what some say is the price of flour now. *4 sous. Lenoir*—he replaced Sartine as the head of police, only to be fired in turn.

Wincing, I reach in and push the pieces around. *Burn. Gallows. Turgot.*

Aimée.

I stare at her name, the pale ink lines smudging and blurring. To what end? To save her? Or to be rid of her?

She had always been a little crude, a little boastful. Never a favorite.

Who among us had made her name glow?

Voices in the hall. Quickly I close the commode, wincing at the smell on my fingers. But as I hurry back to my room, I start to feel a nervous excitement in my belly.

I can make a sigil. Not for myself, I cannot paint my own ceiling, she would suspect me at once.

But I can make a sigil for Isabella.

To love me. To run away with me to the ends of the earth. To feel the same wet desire that I do, to want to taste me as I long to taste her.

To stop Mémé's madness. To make us all safe from that mindless rage.

To love me.

Long into the night I stare at the blank page, I start to write words and stop again. If it takes eight of us just to raise the price of bread, what can I do, alone?

Is it not enough, to simply want to love?

But I think of that mob, and how it would feel to be battered by their clubs and their fists, or helplessly burning as they feed the fire.

I write, then, before I can rethink it, printing the letters atop each other, over and over on scraps of paper until at last I have a drawing that looks like Mémé's.

I tear up the other papers and I lay them in my chamber pot and cover them with my own waters. I will slop them out later, in the far corner of the yard, where the muck gathers just before the drains.

And then I lie in bed, staring at my sigil. *My will.* Staring at the intersection of lines, the moonlight streaming in. *My will upon the universe.* Already my body feels full and heavy. *Isabella.* It is *happening.* My hand between my legs, stroking, rubbing. *My will.* Watching the lines, the paper lit by moonlight as I hold it above my head—

I cry aloud as the sigil flares white, so bright as to blind me, my whole body arching off the bed. Never have I. Never. So much bliss.

The paper on the bed. My palm streaked with rust. Only the fat moon as witness.

Waxing gibbous, Mémé would say.

Almost time.

I am cramping as I dress, breathing through gritted teeth as I wiggle into my gauzy petticoat and draw on my red-clocked stockings, securing them with red ribbons. My feet in slippers. Only then do I lace up the ridiculous stays that stop just below my breasts.

In Mémé's room, she is handing out the buckets,

their brushes swinging gaily inside. That strange cloudy liquid, what is it? Where does it come from? The smell like burying your nose in dirty clothing, sweat and piss and something deeper—

I think of last night, washing my hand after, and I blush. Like *that* smell.

One by one, Mémé hands over the slips of paper, pairing us with a flick of her wrist. "Sophie, for Marie. Jeanne, for Catherine. Isabella, for Claire."

My stomach drops. If Isabella paints my ceiling, how can I paint hers?

To wait another month—

"Catherine, for Louisa. Marie, for Isabella."

I grab the slip instinctively, snatching it from Mémé's hand. Marie looks surprised, and then she smirks at me. "Claire wants to paint herself in Turgot's place," she says slyly, and the others laugh.

"Bite your tongue," I mutter. "I—I thought she said Claire." More giggling.

I have not let go of the paper.

Mémé studies me for a long moment. "It is … unusual," she finally says. "Two marking sigils for each other—but perhaps it will intensify the results?" She nods at the slip in my hand. "Claire, for Isabella. This might be a special night indeed."

Isabella's room smells of her: her odors lie across every surface like dust, and they rise as I move through the space, clinging to me in turn. Her few dresses, the Bible on her nightstand—how is it that she has such a thing? Mémé will not permit so much as a rosary in our rooms.

There but for the grace of God.

I kick off my slippers and climb onto her bed. I paint in quick, strong strokes. I have memorized every line and curve, I know them by heart. For it is my heart I am painting, the picture of my love, the shape of my hope.

Our hand upon the tiller of the world. Or so Mémé said, and I pretended to believe.

And what do I believe now?

I am just finishing when Isabella comes in, surprising me. The brush falls from my hand to her bed, the liquid quickly spreading on the coverlet. At once I snatch it up, not sure where to look, my face burning.

"I didn't mean to startle you," she says.

Still I cannot think. I stumble off her bed. I am trying to gather up the coverlet and keep the bucket and brush to hand, great armfuls of cloth and the bucket swinging wildly. Mémé's slip flutters from my hand to land in the bucket, soaking into the residue. I am scarlet, my ears on fire.

Isabella takes the coverlet from me, wadding it into a ball and shoving it under her bed, and then just stays kneeling on the floor, one hand on my ankle as if to keep me in place.

"Claire," she whispers. "Oh, Claire, they just came …"

I put the bucket down and kneel beside her, carefully putting my hand on her face. Her soft cheek in my palm. I nearly sob aloud, I am so overcome. Still, I draw her face towards mine. Her eyes are full.

"Policemen. I heard Mémé speaking with them. About Aimée." Her tears spilling into my hand. "They found her in the Seine, they say she was not, she wasn't *whole* …"

I hug her tightly, feeling her body shudder against mine as she cries, rubbing her back through the thin silk of her negligee. And if my sigil doesn't work, if she is next to disappear into the crowd, never to come back whole?

"Oh, Claire, Claire," she whispers into my neck. "What if we're making things worse, so much worse?"

"We are making things worse," I say fiercely. "This whole business is madness." Then, in a rush, "If I could get enough money, for us to leave—"

There is a knock on the door, then it swings open. "Mémé's changed the lantern to red," Marie says. "And Turgot is already here. You'll just have to wait your turn, Claire," she adds, sniggering.

Isabella pulls away from me, wiping at her face; when she looks at me again I see not only sorrow and fear in her eyes but a hint of something else, something hard. "I will come to you after," she says.

I will come to you. She has never spoken so before, she has never held me save after my first night. She had come to me after the man left, saying nothing, just holding me until I fell asleep.

I will come to you I will come to you I will come to you

All I can think, as I hurry back to my own room

and quickly rouge my face, douse all but a few candles, arrange myself on the bed—all I can think is that something happened last night. I had made the sigil glow, truly glow, without the energy of a man.

Yet Isabella's words, and all they imply—that wasn't what I had written at all.

I change the sheets after Vergennes leaves, I open the window to the fresh night air. I wash and I comb my hair and I put on my softest, prettiest shift.

But Isabella never comes.

It is early when the knocking rouses me from an uneasy sleep. I think *Isabella*, but instead it is Catherine, looking nervous.

"They brought in emergency flour last night," she says. "The price of bread has dropped to three *sous* four *deniers* and the people are cheering Louis. Mémé is furious, she thinks one of us changed their thing." She shrugs, but keeps her eyes lowered. "More likely we just missed a line. Anyway, she wants us to show her what we painted, and to talk to each of us."

As she speaks I feel my stomach disappear. I cannot remember what Mémé gave me, I had been far too intent on getting my own sigil right. I manage a nod, but as soon as Catherine leaves I drop before my dressing-table, trembling.

I do not fear for myself. What can she do to me in the end? Beat me, turn me out. If she denounces me to the police she risks herself; if she throws me out, I know better how to survive now.

But I know she will never let me see Isabella again.

I make myself dress, swallowing my sobs. Halfway down the stairs I remember: the paper had fallen in the bucket, it might still be there—

But when I hurry to the closet, I find only clean, dry buckets, neatly stacked for next month.

And when I step back into the hall, Mémé is standing in her open doorway. She beckons to me, her strange smooth face expressionless. Her long thin hand, beckoning, as Isabella had beckoned all those months ago.

My choice.

As I enter the room she shuts and locks the door behind us. Isabella is sitting on Mémé's bed and she will not meet my eyes.

"Sit at the desk, Claire," Mémé says.

There is a piece of paper, a pen, an inkwell. The chair creaks beneath me as I sit down. My hands on the polished wood surface. All the drawers are unlocked now, but what does it matter anymore?

"I want you to draw, as best you remember, what you painted on Isabella's ceiling."

In my mind's eye I can see the sigil flaring into life. The pen and ink sit there, waiting to be used.

"And thus hath the candle sing'd the moth." Mémé sighs the words out as the bed creaks beneath her weight. "Claire, Claire. I have never before taken a girl I did not choose myself, but Isabella is special to me. Now I can see I made a mistake."

She strokes Isabella's head. Isabella still won't look at me.

"We are so close, Claire." She takes Isabella's hand and presses it into her own lap. "So close to an uprising that will change all our lives. But I cannot have less than eight each month. Did I not take Aimée's place myself last night, so we could be eight? So we might finish what we began?" She takes a breath. "Yet now, because of you, we were not eight. Because of you, we may lose all that we have worked for. What did you paint on her ceiling?"

"I cannot remember," I say, hoping against hope it sounds like the truth.

Mémé's foot taps on the floor, the tempo increasing with each passing moment—

And then she seizes Isabella by the throat with one hand, a knife in her other, pulling her close and driving the point into Isabella's cheek, just below her eye. Blood wells around the blade and Isabella shrieks in fright, making me cry "No!"

"Draw it," Mémé says calmly. "Draw it or I will cut her face and she will spend the rest of her days servicing men at the quays. Draw it."

"You wouldn't hurt her." I nearly stutter in my panic. "You need her, you need her for Turgot."

"What do I care about Turgot if we fail? And if I am to replace one, I can as easily replace two." She digs the blade deeper and Isabella starts sobbing. "Draw it!"

Choking on my tears, I shove the pen in the ink and draw as fast as I can. The point digging and scratching, the ink splattering. Isabella crying behind me, *oh my love*—

"There," I yell, holding up the paper, smeared and blotched. "That's what I drew! And it didn't work because it's all a ploy, to make us do what other whores won't. We haven't made anything happen, we've changed nothing!"

Mémé shoves Isabella aside and lunges forward, seizing my arm and spinning me face-first onto the floor. Her knee pinning my back, her hand on my neck; she presses down, crushing my face against the wood.

"We'll see what I can change," she cries furiously. "Let's see if I can change *your* world, eh? Yours and hers and anyone else you have turned with your deceit."

I buck and kick but I cannot dislodge her. Something in my nose is cracking and I cannot breathe and I can feel her tensing against my back—

There is a rush of air, a sickening thud, and her weight disappears. I look over my shoulder to see Mémé fallen on her side. I turn over completely and Isabella is holding the poker in her hand, its tip darkly wet. It takes me a moment to realize she is trembling everywhere, her face pale save for the scabbing blood on her cheek.

Mémé's body is still.

I start to crawl towards Mémé. If she is dead, it will be the gallows for us both …

"No," Isabella says hoarsely. "Don't touch her."

I get to my feet, my head throbbing, my nose hot and tender. "We need to get away." I sound as if I am speaking through a tube. "There may be money in her desk."

Isabella only stands there, shaking, her eyes darting from Mémé to me and back again. Carefully I take the poker from her hands, not daring to touch the gouge on her cheek.

Behind us Mémé makes a gurgling sound; we both jump. Still, she lies unmoving.

"I'm so sorry," Isabella whispers then.

"For what? She would have killed us both."

"For bringing you here." She is crying again. "I— I changed your sigil. Claire! I changed your sigil. Only I could not find the words to confess it, she was enraged, it frightened me. But it was me, it was me, I figured out how she made them and I changed yours."

I can only gape at her.

"I changed your sigil," she repeats more slowly. "I couldn't bear it any more, watching them go to you, knowing I did this to you. You were just so beautiful that day, so beautiful and sad, and I thought I could help you, give you some, some food, money, I don't know. And then Mémé thought …" She wipes at her eyes, takes a shuddering breath. "I made it say you would leave Paris, leave and be happy and never again have to do *this*."

"But I changed yours," I say, stupidly.

Isabella falls silent.

"I changed yours. It wasn't that I couldn't remember hers. What I showed her was what I painted. That's why I took the slip from Marie, to be the one to paint your ceiling."

"What did you change it to?" she whispers, her voice nearly inaudible.

"That something would stop her, and you would be safe." I am weeping now, my breath catching in my swollen nostrils. "I know—I know you don't love me, not as I love you, but that day, all the violence and Aimée … it wasn't right that we were making things so terrible. And I thought I could at least free you from her, I could make you safe …"

At once she is in my arms.

4.

There is little here save for rocky beach and scrub to the front, grass and stunted pines behind. The cottage was once the residence of an elderly fisherman—*a hermit*, the villagers tell us, shaking their heads that anyone would want such a decrepit property, only that tiny garden and a barn they wouldn't keep the devil in.

It suits us perfectly.

Every day we listen to the surf; every night we study the fields of stars. We have turned our bed to the east, to face the dawn.

We ordered marigold seeds, giggling together like naughty little girls.

Did the sigils really work? I still cannot say for certain. I had wanted Isabella safe, Mémé stopped, but I had imagined it would come in the form of police, not our own hands. I do know that there were no more mobs after that day, or so we read in the gazettes after. We were away on the first coach.

The fishermen here tell us that a tiller takes a light hand. Perhaps Mémé tried too hard, demanding instead of asking, pushing instead of letting events unfold in their time.

Isabella's body next to mine, embracing me. Her hand sliding over me, inside me. And then rising up again to draw the sigil on my face, lazy strokes of her thumb, the easy slide of her fingertips.

Kissing me, everywhere but where she traced the sigil. Drawing my legs between hers, pressing us together. Her thigh between, her heat against my skin. My mouth dropping to her neck, her breasts, and we are rocking and sliding and then she suddenly cries out, staring into my face, her own suffused with love and I love and oh the light—

We do not demand, we ask. We do not plot, we suggest. No hunger, no suffering, no murderous rage. Just the slightest touch on the tiller, turning the world towards something a little kinder, a little sweeter, a little more like love.

PROPERTIES OF OBLIGATE PEARLS

YOU HAVE to know what to look for. Younger, definitely—stones from the elderly are heavy and black,
decades of layers dulling the luster. No one wants the
weight of a grandmother's worries around their neck.

Take the young woman sitting across from me. I
saw her in the supermarket, late on Friday night. She
should have been out partying, or on a date; instead
she was pushing a cart that was equal parts cat food,
stew meat, and adult diapers. Everything about her
spoke of exhaustion and embarrassment.

Even under her jacket I could glimpse the fullness
of her torso, that hint of bloating directly beneath her
sternum.

She was stooped and tired and looked older than
she was, but she was also lovely. That's part of it, too
—you can get a decent stone from a lot of people, but
sometimes they have this hint of beauty about them,
like a smothered light. Those stones have a little extra

luster, a greater range of hues, and that can make all the difference.

I followed her home that night. I came back the next morning, before dawn, and watched her go to work, then to the hospital, then hurry home again. The neighbors said she was both caring for a father and helping her brother with some kind of treatment. That, and the father was nutty about his cats, their little apartment was full of the beasts.

It was no wonder, then, that when I asked her to lunch she accepted with a robotic *sure*. She probably couldn't remember her last full night of sleep, much less have any instincts about going to lunch with a strange woman dressed in a suit.

"It's a particular kind of condition," I explain patiently, while she wolfs down her poached fish. "You have all the symptoms: bloodshot sclera, poor sleep, bloating and tenderness, yellowing fingernails, hair loss …"

"And you'll pay me 50,000 to take it out?" she asks between mouthfuls.

"If it's indeed the right kind of tumor, yes. We're desperate for specimens to study." I smile then, sympathetically. "I know it's not a great deal of money, and there's always a slight risk with surgery …"

"No, no, I'm definitely interested." She gulps down her wine and leaned in close, clearly buzzed. "It would make such a difference to us, you have no idea."

Oh, I have an idea. I have more than an idea.

But I say nothing as it comes pouring out. How her mother died suddenly and her father subsequently deteriorated. How her brother had been helping until *he* got sick, and the treatments are working but they're experimental, they're not covered … Oh, she doesn't mind doing so much, truly she doesn't, only the cats —! Her father refuses to give them up but half of them don't get along with the other half, they're always making noise, sometimes she just wants to strangle them all … Meanwhile she was passed over for a raise for poor performance, and she doesn't know where the money's all going, she budgets down to the last cent and somehow she always comes up short …

Listening, I've learned, is a lot like meditation. You have to observe the litany without reacting to it. I used to react: I used to hold their hands and offer suggestions; I used to weep for them, with them.

I used to weep for myself.

But in the end, all our stories are the same unsolvable conundrum: money that doesn't stretch far enough and the overwhelming needs of others. It's the latter that's key. People who have personal crises produce tumors without centers. It's the obligations that make it happen, that somehow gunk up the fluids into something small, hard, and incredibly beautiful.

Obligate pearls.

She comes on her day off, having told the brother she

needed to care for the father and vice versa. She dresses up for it. A lot of them do, as if their appearance will affect their payout. When the tests come back positive she takes the gown we give her and then cries in the privacy of the operating room, sobs of relief that carry through the door. The money never really changes anything, though; having more of it only means it stretches a little further for a while. Budgets are like rubber bands—sooner or later they always snap back into the same tight, mean shape as before.

I've been doing this long enough now that I'm starting to get people coming back to me, but I've never tried a second extraction. Instinct tells me it'll be more like the granny pearls: dull, black things. Something about losing hope a second time.

The surgery goes smoothly enough, as well it should, considering how many times I've done it. The woman is healthy and Ana, my perpetually somber nurse, never misses a beat. Soon enough I've got a small lump of flesh in a tray and I'm sewing the woman back up while Ana washes the lump clean and pats it dry, like a piece of meat. Then she wheels the woman out into the adjacent room to wake up and starts putting together her recovery kit: painkillers, instructions on cleaning the sutures, who to call if something goes wrong (not me), and 50,000 in two fat envelopes. I used to handle the recoveries, but there was something about how they looked, after: some kind of hollow shock, though they never said anything other than to thank me. Easier to let Ana deal with it.

Only when I have the operating room to myself do I turn my attention to the tray. I fit the pick onto my thumb—it's a little apparatus of my own design, a few guitar picks fused together and the edge carefully shaped, then attached to a ring. With this I start digging into the tissue, without fear of scratching the stone inside. At last I feel that little click as the plastic touches its surface, and I start cutting away the outer layers until I can work the pearl free.

Before me sits three years of anxiety and grief, its surface shimmering opalescent beneath the fluorescent lights, its colors shifting from a powdery blue to a near-violet cast, the whole thing the size of a gumball. So much sadness. So much disappointment.

They say wearing one relieves you of your own sorrows. The pearl continues to build layers through contact, siphoning off your fears and anxieties, your sorrow and grief. As always, I'm tempted to keep it and put the theory to the test. To sleep through the night again, to move through the day without that small fluttering panic in my belly? To not feel like everything, *everything* is eggshell-fragile, and my slightest mistake will shatter it all?

Oh, I'm tempted. But as always, the money wins out.

It's too late to sell the pearl tonight so I bring it home with me instead. Even on the short journey from my office, I could *feel* it, feel myself becoming a little more empty, as if I'd had a good cry on the bus back here.

Or am I just imagining it?

In what had been our bedroom, Dana is sitting propped up in bed watching the silent television, and I relax a little. The last nurse we had insisted on a regular bedtime, regardless of whether I was home or not, which always agitated him. He likes to wait up for me, likes to make sure I get home safely.

His face is grey with pain, and even as I kiss him, I'm checking his levels, but they're right where they should be.

"Think I've built up my tolerance again," he wheezes.

I open up the drip a little before curling up in the bed next to him, wadding my coat to pad his bony shoulder. I can no longer remember how he felt before he got sick, save for flashes of a firm, muscular bicep, the pillow of a healthy belly. I'm losing him, little by little, moment by moment. It makes my stomach knot, and I try to focus instead on the screen before us where a woman is defiantly striding out of a house, flinging her wedding ring into the hydrangeas as she leaves.

"Was it a good one?"

I hold the pearl up before him. He touches it, stroking its smooth surface. It seems to turn a shade darker, though it's probably just a trick of the light. Still, I wrap it in a tissue before slipping it back into my pocket.

"After I sell it," I tell him, "I'll see the doc about

something stronger." Though I'm not sure what's left to try; I'm not sure there is anything left to try. But Dana nods without protesting, which tells me it must be bad.

"Do you want me to open it up more?"

"I'm all right," he says, though his jaw is rigid. Then, "Your mother called, before. Left a message 'for my daughter Rachel.' Old bat's getting bolder."

"I'll talk to her."

"Like hell you will." He moves his hand over mine. "You do you, babe. Talking to her's brought you nothing but grief."

I say nothing, but I press closer to him, squeezing his hand as much as I dare with the IV.

"You're beautiful, Ray," he wheezes. "*We're* beautiful. Anyone says otherwise, send 'em to me."

My throat is pin-tight. If I start speaking now I'll just start crying, which will only upset him in turn. I reach for his other hand, closing my fingers over his. On the screen the woman is driving away as the credits roll, into open countryside bathed in sunlight. Dana can't bear to leave me alone and vulnerable; I can't bear to hurt him by telling him to go. So we linger here, spending every cent on painkillers and medications, prolonging the inevitable. There isn't a pearl big enough to take it all away. Not even my own.

My dealer calls herself Babette but Dana calls her Madame B. She's a Madame kind of woman, the kind you can't imagine as anything but her polished middle-aged self, the kind you can't imagine owning a pair of sweatpants. *Pearls*, she told me when I started out, *are a woman's game. Men never know how to handle them right, just as a pearl from a man always fetches less than one from a woman. They lack a certain depth, a grief without name.*

Which is bullshit. I've sold her pearls from men before and lied about it, and she never remarked on some kind of missing mystical grief. But she knows her stones—and she's got the clientele to buy them. As long as I've been doing this, she's had a near-monopoly on the market.

She sizes up my latest now, loupe stuck in her eye, fingers stroking the surface. At last she nods with satisfaction. "A stunning one. I'll give you 300 for it."

"400," I say. She'll get 500 for it easy, perhaps more if she puts it in a fancy setting, or if she already has a buyer lined up. And she usually has a buyer lined up.

She makes a face at me but I fold my arms. I need the 400, and I'm her best source now. The others are all teams, one to choose the person, one to do the surgery, but there's something about doing it all yourself, about seeing the whole process through, from selection to open wound, from outer implication to inner truth.

"Very well," she sighs, "but you're robbing me." She digs into her desk drawer and starts laying out bundles marked *100 000*. "You're not paying out more, are you?" When I shake my head, she exhales.

"Good, because I think our little enterprise might truly be coming to an end, Ray. First that exposé, and now a group of psychiatrists has started putting out feelers—legal extractions with a guaranteed payment. Only for small ones, mind you, but it's only a matter of time. I hope you've been socking it away."

I feel suddenly as if I'm in a tunnel, everything hollow and echoing. Something must have shown on my face, because she asks more quietly, "No improvements, then?"

I swallow hard, and again. "No," I finally manage.

"You know it's true, about these." She holds the pearl up to the light. "That's why the shrinks are so keen. A client the other day told me the trick is to wear it below your breasts, where your own would grow? Do that for a night and you wake up feeling like you've wept for days. That empty feeling, like everything's been washed away."

"I don't think it would work for me," I say, rubbing beneath my breasts.

"I wasn't thinking about you," she says. Before I can reply she continues, "So how much will you want for yours? Dana's been ill for, what, three, four years now? It's worth 400 at least, probably more, minus whatever you'd have to pay for the extraction of course. Sam's probably your best bet for that, his hands are good. It's just his eye that's shitty."

I can't think of what to say. Months of quiet panic, of everything feeling like eggshells, waiting to reach this precipice; yet now that it's come I feel utterly blindsided.

Madame B looks at the pearl, rolling it between her fingers. "I've been thinking I might keep yours, you know," she says. "For the personal connection."

"I can't see that you need one," I mutter. I'm still rubbing my torso. I have this urge to cover the spot with my hands, like a child.

But she only laughs, soft and bitter. "Oh, my dear Ray," she says. "I've never met a person who didn't. I'm no exception; I'm the rule."

I lie in bed that night next to Dana, who's sleeping at last, as peacefully as he can these days. His face is exhausted in the dim light of the monitors, jaw still clenched with pain. The last painkiller we haven't yet tried. After this it's back to the beginning, going through the list again … and his meds are "temporarily unavailable," no one can tell us what that even means, but we cannot waste a dose until they come in next week, and there will be new side effects now, and how much more of it all can he even take …

The pearl money all but gone now.

I press and press at my torso, teasing out the faint curve beneath my skin. Just the hint of a presence. I can't even see it save from certain angles. The shock when I first discovered it. So many times I'd been told *I never knew I had this* and thought it impossible. I figured they must feel something, they just didn't know what. But here I was utterly unaware of it.

What does my pearl look like? Whose sorrows will it feed on, when it ceases to feed on mine?

Beside me Dana mumbles, "If I wasn't here to look after you, what would you do?"

I look at him but his eyes are closed, his breathing regular. Talking in his sleep. And I want to ask him, I want to awaken him and ask him if the question was rhetorical, or does he want me to answer?

"It's the nature of the game," Sam says expansively. "We knew this day would come, didn't we? It was just a matter of how long we could ride the gravy train for. I'll be damned if I'm going back to the hospital, though. Plenty of other work for a good surgeon, if you're not fussy about what you do."

We're sitting at lunch, at a restaurant he chose. It's chic and expensive and I'm eating a salad and drinking tap water. I've put my only dress on because I know the suits annoy Sam. As it is, he can't keep from grimacing every time his eyes alight on my crew-cut. I need him to help me, not be repulsed by me.

After all, he has the best hands in this business. Better than mine.

"Still, you've done all right for yourself, haven't you? Babette never shuts up about you." He cuts into his meat, raises it rare and dripping to his mouth, and chews thoughtfully. "She even thinks she can tell yours apart," he continues around his mouthful. "In society photos and the like. Always pointing them out to me.

That's one of Rachel's, you can tell by the size, by the glow they have."

I have to swallow my response; we both know full well Madame B would never use that name, not anymore. "I need to know if you'll do this for me," I say.

"What's to keep me from keeping yours?"

"I've already told Babette, and no one else will give you as much for it."

"Of course, of course. Just making sure you have a buyer, and I'll get my fee." He lays his cutlery down and taps at his wristband, eyeing the projected calendar. "So, perhaps, say, Thursday morning—"

"End of the day," I interrupt. "As soon as possible."

"If we do it in the morning, you'll have time to recover and then see her—"

"End of the day," I repeat. "At my office. I'll go home that night and bring it to her in the morning. It's how I do things." When he looks at me with the grimace, I sigh and explain, "I want to show Dana before I sell it."

"Ah, of course. How is dear Dana?"

"He's dying," I say, and get up before he can say anything more.

There is nothing stranger than being on your own table. At last seeing what the others saw, all those tired people, looking up with hope and trepidation. I am looking up with hope and trepidation. I don't think Sam will do anything, but he's always been far more cutthroat about it all—and while Madame B is powerful, she's not here. If I die on the table, there's nothing she can do about it.

I told Ana: if anything goes wrong, just go along with Sam until you can get away, then go to Madame B. Make her pay you something. This is as much her idea as mine, she can pay out and chase Sam for the pearl. Make her pay enough that Dana has a choice at least. About how to go forward, about how to end it all.

He won't leave me because he thinks I need him and I can't let him go because he needs me to need him and I need him to love me and I can't bear to hurt him, I can't—

But maybe I can take something away, enough to let us both do what must be done.

And when I awaken I'm utterly, utterly empty. I feel like I've been hollowed out; I hardly feel anything at all. In the tray Sam holds out to me is a massive pearl as blue as twilight and as lustrous as silk, and I think, *that's the closest thing I'll ever have to a soul. The damn thing is everything* but *my obligations.*

It's late when I come home. Dana's half-asleep, the

television flashing images of vacation paradises with a muted commentary, the glow painting his drawn face in sharp relief. I take a moment to look, to really look at him, before I slip off my shoes and painfully ease myself onto the bed, nudging aside the tubes and wires that surround him like a nest.

He stirs, and I sense the effort it takes for him to turn his head, to lift his hand enough to touch my arm.

"That kind of a day," he rasps.

I nod, careful to keep my bandages hidden. Instead I take his hand and nestle the pearl in it.

And there are things I had thought to say now. Stuff about how this pearl is different, stuff about how he doesn't have to worry. Stuff about what will become of me once he's gone, that everything will be okay.

Stuff about how he can let go now.

But all I can think of is the awful, aching emptiness in my belly, so I merely close his fingers over the pearl and press his fist to his sternum, just below his breasts.

"Nicest one yet," he whispers. "Beautiful, like you."

"Like us," I say, but the words sound hollow.

It takes a while, but at last I feel it: his body softening against mine, the tension in his face easing. He sighs deeply, a shuddering breath, and I think he's about to cry but he only relaxes more. I open up the drip completely and he sleeps at last, truly sleeps, and I doze as well, sliding in and out of awareness, and we're no longer pressed together on the narrow bed but lying on a twilit beach, *not a care in the world*, the television whispers. Lying twined together in silky-soft sand, *not a care in the world*, slowly sliding down, down into a cool, damp darkness that wraps around us like a shroud.

SABBATHS

SHE HAD LEFT the firewood the day before, trundling the wheelbarrow back and forth under the cool dawn sky, before anyone would be on the road to see her. Now she gathered their things: a half-dozen charms and rings, bound hair shorn rough at the end, pieces of lace and embroidered handkerchiefs, the locket and the reticule. She put them all in the big market basket with the candle stub and the match-box, wedged the grimoire over them and piled apples on top of that, and with the wineskin slung over her shoulder, she started walking.

It was twilight. The dirt road was a grey ribbon between the cornfields; a few last crows cawed their farewells. Over the rise until their little cottage was out of sight. Forty paces further was the indent marked with the striped rock. There, she stepped off the road and into the cornfield and its ghosts.

Striped rocks were lucky, that was one of the first

things they had taught her. Only they had never specified what kind of luck, good or bad.

In the cornfields all was memory. Memory guided her steps, though she could not see the way; memory turned her rustling passage into the soft laughter of past nights, the voices caught by the breeze as they, too, marched through the corn, following their own markings. Memory transmuted the rasp of the leaves on her bare arm into the slide of Ellie's fingernails as she caught at her, giggling breathless, *slow down, you know I cannot keep up!*

She slowed down. She would always slow down.

A wind came out of nowhere, bowing the stalks before her, and in the deepening gloaming she saw not swaying corn but the gentle swinging of the bodies beneath the gallows, and the basket handle in her hand was the rope as she sawed away at it.

From her left came Hannah's deep voice: *They won't ever come for us. They wouldn't dare.*

From her right came Margery, laughing as usual: *Too worried we'll hex their cocks off!* All the field laughing then, laughing and singing

A little love may prove a pleasure
Too great a passion is a pain

And even Ellie too, though she always sang quieter, because she was embarrassed to be singing about such things.

That hint of embarrassment—once it would have set her burning with desire. Now she only felt a coldness in the pit of her stomach at the memory, a hard clenching and the first hint of tears, and she stopped completely in the corn, the basket sliding to her feet. *Ellie*, she whispered aloud, and the corn rustled with approval. *Ellie. Ellie.* The name a charm in her mouth. She kept saying it over and over until it was just sounds, and then took up her basket once more.

Closer to the edge the corn began to thin and now she glimpsed the clearing, right between corn and forest, where the world of men and the world of the wild rubbed uneasily against each other. As she reached to push aside the last stalk she felt, as always, that she became two people, herself now and herself then, the first time she had come. Young and straining in a body that had become a prison, all blooming curves and at every turn restriction, restriction, skirts suddenly twice their length and so hot she had fainted, stomach bound until there was no room for food, her house a cell she could not exit without permission. Until she had seen the distant glow of the bonfire from her window and snuck out into the corn, searching by sound and smell in the darkness, and when she had pushed the corn apart that circle of smiles had turned to her, their bodies wonderfully naked and lips stained with wine, and they had to a one opened their arms and said *welcome sister*.

She pushed aside the corn now and there was nothing but the clearing, a circle of trampled earth with a blackened center upon which she has carefully arranged the wood. *The navel of this world*, Ellie had explained, sitting shyly beside her, *and the fire is like the cord, you see? So we come here to nourish our souls.* And she had on impulse taken Ellie's hand in her own and nothing had ever felt so right …

Slowly, she dropped into a crouch at the edge of the circle, letting the basket and wineskin slide from her body, letting it all slide into the welcoming earth.

Each month it took longer. Longer to rest after the long walk through the corn, longer to arrange the objects in their places. There could be no fire before readiness, so she stumbled around the circle with the flickering candle stub, her world reduced to that small pool of light and beyond it the darkness and the ghosts. Hannah, Margery, Agatha, Janet, the two Roses, Norah and Gladys, Sarah and Alice. Her own Ellie. With herself they had been twelve, a good, strong number. She fancied she could feel Ellie's small hand in hers, helping her along, fiddling with her arrangements, so that the ring she had placed where Norah sat was suddenly propped up on a pebble and Alice's fichu was neatly folded.

She fancied she saw them all out of the corner of her eye, crowded deep in the shadows of the trees, but when she turned completely there were only the trees and the corn.

She fancied that Ellie forgave her.

And then she touched the candle to the kindling and set the world alight, as bright as day. The navel of the world, the cord of light rising to the heavens, and she longed to somehow seize it and draw it down, down, to the earth and its horrors and put her face to it and demand, why have you done these things to us?

But she knew that wasn't how it worked; that had never been how it worked.

She stripped off her worn dress with ease, slipping feet out of shoes and wadding her stockings and bloomers into the basket. The night air set her skin alight with gooseflesh. She took care with the grimoire, keeping all the notes and letters in their places. There was something in its annotations, something that made it greater than the sum of its words. As they had been greater together. Her voice was thin as she read the opening prayer, but in her ears it became doubled with Hannah's booming recital, the consonants made drumbeats, the slide of the vowels tugging their bodies into movement.

She read the prayer, and she danced and sang and danced more. Sometimes she stumbled, but she kept her mouth open and her body moving. In her mind's eye she saw the flames and her voice and the tremors of her movements all rising into the night, twining and drifting, and how others might go to the window as she had once done and feel the pull of that strange glow, restless girls and women heavy with exhaustion and care, they too feeling as if their bodies, their very lives were calcifying around them like a cocoon of stone.

She saw all this, and she saw the men who might see the great cord rising, and how it might be they who come through the corn as they had that night, so that when the circle turned smiling with open arms it had been to a mob armed with pistols and bare-teethed rage, and how the fire had sputtered just at that moment, tumbling back to the earth as if neatly snipped in two. Hannah and Norah seized before they could flee, Ellie panting frantic beside her as they ran naked through the corn, the leaves cutting their bodies and the earth drinking their blood. For months after in the whole of the county there had been bodies upon bodies, bodies accused and denounced, bodies tried and condemned, bodies cut down from gallows and dragged sodden from lakes, scraped up as bone and ash and prised rotting from gutters with a hand-kerchief over her mouth. The relentless fear and horror, day after day, month after month, season after season, until her nerves jangled at every sound and she lay awake every night, wide with terror. Until she had felt worn to the point where she was simply fear, nothing more.

Had she gone mad from it? She thought so now, for how else to explain how she came to be standing on a strange man's doorstep one dawn, saying *not us, not Ellie and I*, and he had looked her over with visible disgust and agreed *not you*. The names tripping over her tongue as if fighting to get out. Rose and Rose, Janet, Gladys, Agatha, Sarah and Alice, Margery. Shivering on his threshold for he would not let her through the door, as if her very being was a curse.

When they had come for Ellie, she had risen to join her and the men had said *not you*, and had left her too stunned to weep.

Not you, not you. She sang the phrase like the curse that it was, and she drank heavily of the wine and she danced. Twelve had been a good number, a strong number. Above her the heavens were alight with the glow, and she felt her body become more limber, her voice stronger in her throat until it was like the baying of an animal, freed for one more night, *oh Ellie my Ellie, not you, not you,* and she waited to see what would come out of the corn.

THE QUEEN OF LAKES

WHEN MY BROTHER and I were small enough to share a bedroom without embarrassment, our mother read to us at night. She had an old book of stories that her mother had given her, before they left Scotland— tales of princes and knights facing great perils. Even when she began with a swineherd, or a lowly apprentice, Tim and I knew at once that the boy was secretly of noble blood, perhaps even royalty. The heroes of Mother's stories always fought alone, no matter the odds. They slew each-uisges and great sea monsters, outwitted kelpies and trowes; they stayed deaf to the calls of selkies and banshees. At the end, they triumphantly claimed their spoils: rooms full of treasure, kingdoms to rule, and the most beautiful maidens for their brides.

Afterwards, when Mother's voice had faded with the candlelight, when her lips had brushed our foreheads and her cracked, callused hands had smoothed down our blankets, I would fall asleep and enter a bright world full of heat and color and blood. Sweltering in my armor, the gory head of a creature skewered on my sword, the roar of a thousand voices all cheering *me*. And then to the tower, kicking open the door and climbing the cool stone stairs, until I come at last to the enchanted chamber, where my princess silently awaits her king.

King Rose.

I didn't understand, you see. That only men could quest, and fight, and triumph.

Every day Mother wakes me to a world grey with exhaustion. I braid my hair in the dark, listening to Father snoring. A bit of bread and some cold tea and I am out the door and into a silvery dawn. I imagine I am rising in time with the sun, both of us jostled out of our beds, trudging towards our circumstances. We work all day, the sun and I, my back aching and my eyes straining to see the thread against the cloth.

If the sun did not rise, I would not have to go, but I don't know how to make it my conspirator. Who tells the sun what to do?

With each step the sky lightens, trees forming out of the gloom. Amidst their skeletal forms, I can make out patches of early snow, tinted pink. My breath makes a raspy sound, like I am old before my time. I *am* old before my time. There is the forest and the road weaving through and my plodding feet lumpish in my woolen stockings and clogs. If I close my eyes I can see exactly how I look: small and dumpling-plump in my layers, my scarf low over my head to cover my ears, only my chapped face visible.

My nose is running.

When the road begins to curve, the start of a wide, blind arc leading over a rise, I do not dare quicken my pace. But my breath quickens: it comes in short, loud pants.

At the crest of the rise I can see it, its surface scummed with algae and ice. The lake is wide and deep, and even in winter you cannot see the far bank. It seems to run to the very horizon; it seems without end. When I was small people fished here, Father included, and things were better then. In those days, I had hoped to finish school, perhaps even go to the city like Tim did, to train as a teacher. *Miss Rose.*

But there was a girl of marrying age, and then a boy, and then another girl, all found dead on the banks of the lake. When they found the first girl, everyone thought it the work of an animal, but the lake began to smell, and the fish became thin and small, *not even worth cleaning* Mother said.

Three long days passed between the boy disappearing and his remains being found. Abigail Fitzwilliam said she saw his body all torn to pieces, though I knew she was just repeating something she overheard. She could never bear to see even a drop of blood.

That night, Mother and Father stayed up late, whispering, and though I could not make out all the words, I remember hearing Mother say *it's almost like that daft story of Gran's, about that man-horse creature. The each-uisge.*

And Father said something sharp and growling, his tone so enraged it made me shudder to hear it, and the next day the story book was gone.

When the second girl disappeared, Mr. Duggan came to tell us. I remember Mother crying and then looking at me hard, as if I had something to do with it. Later, Abigail told me the girl had been *loose*, which made me envision a doll with its joints all broken, its limbs flailing wildly. No wonder she had come apart in pieces.

Three deaths in all. For weeks after, Father would go out at night with other men, carrying torches and rifles and axes, and Bart Masterson with his blunderbuss. Even when it was all right to walk past the lake again, things were never the same. There were no more fish in the water, no more birds in the trees. Slowly the soil began to grow dry and crumbled, as if some poison were leaching out from the lake itself. From my window, I could watch the grey color overtake the rich brown, a few feet each year, the crops rising green on one side, stunted and withering on the other, until we had only a cartful of surplus to bring to market.

Each summer, a strange odor came from the lake, like that of a dead animal.

And still the sun sat in the sky, and Tim went to university with all our money for his fees, and I was taken out of school and told I had to sew for Mrs. Duggan, every day now for months, and it seemed that it might be this way for the rest of my life, either piecework or marriage to Bart Masterson's oldest boy Sam, doing for him and lying beneath his oafish smirk.

Every day, up before dawn. Every day, the needle or Sam Masterson. Until last month, when the each-uisge came back.

The moment the path starts to dip, the world goes silent. The very wind ceases to blow, not a leaf stirs, not an animal can be seen, not even an insect. There is only the rasp of my breath, the blood thudding in my ears.

It is forty-two steps from the silence to the far end of the curve. Forty-two steps where the only sound in the world is myself.

Myself and the each-uisge, I mean.

"Where did you go?" I ask. For he is beside me, though I did not hear him approach. I never hear him.

"Here and there," he gurgles. His voice is low and wet, as if his mouth were full of jelly. "Across great lakes and little rivers, so many lovely sights. Though not a one as lovely as you, Rose."

He teases my braid, making it sticky and knotted, and I slap his hand away. Thanks to his fondling, I've been scolded by Mrs. Duggan more than once now, for looking slovenly. He strokes the bare strip of my throat instead, smearing my skin as he hooks a gluey finger beneath my scarf, trying to tug it away from my neck.

His fingers are so very cold.

The first time he touched me I was so frightened, I nearly stopped walking, but I didn't stop. I have never stopped.

I don't know what will happen if I stop.

"Shall I tell you all the places I have been, Rose?" His breath smells of moss. "Would you like that? To hear about the world? Would that please you?"

His hands drop to my chest, rubbing my breasts through the thick wool of my coat. Moisture seeps into the fabric; still he slides his hands in slow circles. No boy has ever touched me like this. The sensation makes strange muscles flex between my legs.

My feet have not stopped moving: twenty-three, twenty-four, twenty-five steps.

"You know it would," I whisper.

He raises his hands and lays them over my eyes. His palms gum my lids shut; his long torso presses against my backside. We are still walking, but we are somewhere else now: we are in a world vibrant with color, warm and rich, filled with the smells of good earth and blossoming flowers. Everywhere I see handsome, well-dressed people, men and women, all laughing and talking and reading. *Reading.* He slithers against my buttocks, up and down, up and down, but I can only see the books and papers, the gazettes and broadsheets, their warm smiles as they share their words with each other.

"Come with me, Rose," he says. "Come with me and see for yourself."

I am panting like a winded horse. He rubs faster now, whining in my ear—

—and then he exhales, long and whistling.

"Oh, Rose," he sighs. "No books in the Masterson house, my sweet girl, not even a Bible." His icy tongue laps at my earlobe. "And you do know this sewing is making you blind?"

Forty-two. The rush of the world in my ears: whistling winds, cawing birds, the scuttling of rabbits and squirrels while the trees rustle and creak. I wipe and wipe at my eyes, flicking away clots of opaque muck. The wet patches on my breasts and backside are already drying; still I feel moisture on my face. It takes me a moment to realize I am weeping.

At Mrs. Duggan's we make clothes for a shop in the city. An older woman does the cutting and each girl does a different part, a main seam or a bit of finer work, say hemming or turning a collar. I sew button-holes and Abigail sews buttons—she's a clumsy girl, thick-fingered, but her father deals in lumber so she only works for her own pin money.

Buttonholes are slow, difficult work. In the summer, the light is good but the heat wrinkles the cloth and makes my palms sweaty. In the winter, the light is so thin I find myself with my face in the cloth, squinting. My dreams now are of an accident:

another girl nudges my chair, or Abigail leans in suddenly, and my hand slips; the last thing I see is the needle aimed for my eye. And then I awaken, sweating with terror, not at the pain but at the *dark*.

"Your Tim not coming for the holidays?"

I blink my eyes rapidly until they can focus on Abigail's plump, rosy face, and shake my head. Not for my birthday, not for the holidays, perhaps not ever again.

All his promises. I can't even think about it.

"Pity," Abigail says. "But good on him, getting accepted to university. Your mother must be so proud." She smiles at her button with its big, wide shank.

Abigail has a good demeanor, Rose. You could do worse than to emulate her. So Mrs. Duggan tells me; so everyone tells me. *She's always so cheerful.* And the greatest virtue of all: *I've never heard her complain a day in my life.*

"It makes you wonder, though." Abigail laughs. "How did he come up so bright? Look at us, a bunch of lumps to the one. You'd never think we'd produce someone with real learning."

"Speak for yourself," I snap. The other girls pause in their stitching to watch us, but I don't care. "I got him accepted. I wrote his bloody essays, I did his proofs. It was all *me*. And as soon as he's settled, I'm going to join him and start my own studies." I cannot see the shirt on my lap for my rising tears. "The only damn lump in this room is you," I finish bitterly. "So speak for yourself, Abigail Fitzwilliam."

There is silence, then a muffled tittering. A voice says in a too-loud whisper, "I didn't realize we were working with Lady Muck."

"Well," Abigail says, as if we're having a conversation, "I hear he's courting a magistrate's daughter, and he's going abroad to work for a great lawyer. I'm sure he'll look after you once he's married." She smiles at her needle. "Though, of course, by then Sam Masterson will be looking after you, so you won't need to burden anyone."

Another rush of giggles and whispering. I feel like I might scream. *Sam Masterson.* They were my compositions, my proofs. Tim was always slow to understand, he mixed words up and he could never *see* geometry, he could never transpose the equations into shapes. Even now, a year out of school, I know at a glance when a merchant tries to rook Mother, I can do the addition in my head quicker than he can write up the bill, and then I tug her sleeve and she makes him review the prices and I am always right.

I'll send my books to you as I finish them. Tim on his last night home, pale and nervous, as well he should have been. *That way you can keep up while I find out what schools there are for women, and a good boarding house.*

And then he went away.

There were many letters at first, carefully addressed to all of us, never replying to my panicked missives. *Tim, please, they've taken me out of school. At least if I was working in the city, I could make more, enough to pay for my own lessons. Can I not come to you? Tell me what I should do.*

Tim, help me.

Instead we learned about the latest fashions, his new friends. One was a magistrate's son and there was a pretty sister and the father said he had great promise and did we have anything to spare for a better suit, so he would not feel ashamed at their table? Father beaming as he counted out our few saved coins. *My boy, courting a magistrate's daughter! Eating off silver, drinking wine with every meal!*

Tim, help me!

And then, two months ago, the package arrived. There was a long letter, explaining he was going abroad for a term: Sophie's father had arranged for him to clerk for a solicitor. The experience would help him go straight into the best firm once he had his degree. Oh, and Sophie had suggested a present for Rose, a belated birthday gift.

I had recognized the shape at once, that firm, solid rectangle. I had all but snatched it from Father, had ripped the paper wrapping to shreds in my excitement. What could it be? Latin, perhaps, or natural philosophy? Breathlessly I turned it over and read the spine:

The Frugal Housewife

My boy, courting a magistrate's daughter! My boy, eating off silver! My boy, touring Europe!

My boy my boy my boy

I eat dinner alone that day, all the girls shunning me, huddling around Abigail instead. I weep all afternoon, quietly, my tears pattering onto the cloth. Two months and it still hurts so much. *The Frugal Housewife*. Abroad for a term, he would not be back until midsummer at the earliest, he could not say just when he might visit.

Did he throw my letters away? Did he burn them?

I hold my hand up to my face, move it a distance away, then close again, watching my fingers slide in and out of focus. I have no more time.

The Frugal Housewife.

Perhaps I'll have to make my own economies, now.

"Rose," the each-uisge says, his clammy arm draped around my shoulders. "Sweet Rose, I'm so very lonely without you."

I am counting my steps, trying to think. Eight, nine. There is another way to and from the Duggans', but it is long and winding, down to the village road and around. It would mean rising earlier, the whole journey in darkness, it would mean coming back to cold suppers and still the chores to do. All that precious sleep, lost.

And for once, I want to see him.

"Why did you come back?" I ask.

"Why, to see you, of course." He nuzzles at my

ear, smearing his face against my hair. "How has my poor Rose fared all these years, with her family of numbskulls and Sam Masterson ogling her tits? Do any of them even see her, really see her?"

"'All these years?'" I whisper.

"Such long, long years. But I knew from the moment I saw you: you were a girl worth waiting for." He pulls at my coat, peering down at my chest, then laughs as I shove his hand away. "My darling Rose. What does a smart girl like you say to those idiots? All they know is to count the days until some farmboy sticks them full of cock and makes their bellies swell. What does a girl like you say to girls like them?"

Nothing, nothing. Their turned backs were almost a relief today, to be spared their teasing: they've started calling me Missus Masterson, they tell me how lucky I am, he's sown his oats so he'll be ready to settle down.

I'm never sure which phrase makes me more ill, *Missus Masterson* or *settle down*. I am Rose. And I haven't even begun.

"You were never meant for this," he says, his fingers trailing slime down my cheek. "I knew it the moment I saw you. You were meant to be a great woman. You were meant to be a queen—*my* queen."

"A king," I blurt out. *King Rose.* I have not thought of those story-dreams in so long. Now they rush through me, quick and hot, quicker and hotter than his hands that are everywhere and nowhere, doing strange things to the layers of my clothes. And on the heels of the rush comes a last burst of miserable sorrow as I see Tim in my mind's eye, poncing about his college in the suit I bought him, the qualifications I gave him.

"Why not a queen? There are queens who have ruled, Rose. Did no one teach you this? I have whole books about such queens." His hand encircles my wrist. "Come with me and see, Rose. Come with me and I will sit at your feet while you read, and then I will take the book from your hands and undo your dress, button by button."

"The better for you to kill me," I cry, wrenching my hand free.

He steps before me, stopping us.

I have never stopped before. I have never truly *seen* him before. A thick cloudy liquid covers him from head to toe; his skin beneath is a greenish-grey. His face bony and long-jawed, framed by a tangle of dark hair and water-weeds. Still he looks like a man, he wears the clothes of a man. But his eyes are a flat, solid black and the teeth flashing in his lipless mouth are small and sharp and crowded together.

"Never you, Rose. Never you." His voice, his teeth. His *eyes*. "I saw your face that day. I *saw* you. The way you looked at that beastly boy's body, while they wrung their hands and averted their eyes. A queen amongst the rabble."

And I see it: the boy's body on the mossy ground, grey and bloated, the flesh bitten and ravaged. I had felt no fear or shame, just an overwhelming need to touch him, to understand what had happened, what mouth made such injuries, what that boy-flesh had tasted like—

I shove the each-uisge aside and run.

"Rose," he calls after me. "I can free you, don't you *see*?"

It was I who told Abigail about the boy's body, describing the great tears and gouges. Breathless with excitement, fired with my own courage. How had I forgotten? She had burst into tears and told her father, who told mine. I had been whipped for it, and I had hated Father and Abigail both.

"Don't be afraid, Rose." His plaintive voice became small and distant. "Let me free you. Let me free—"

And then he is cut off, and I am in the world once more.

I stop again, trying to calm my racing heart. My head spins with memories: Father whipping me, the long hot strokes on my thighs. His tears, his shouting: to stay home, to do what I'm told to do, to never misbehave, to know my place. How had I forgotten? Too sore to sit at school the next day, all their eyes on me as I stood in the corner. Abigail wide-eyed with her own solemn righteousness, as if she hadn't betrayed me.

With a last, deep breath I straighten my clothes, smooth my hair.

Rose!

The voice makes me jump. Never have I heard him here, in the world. My mind is playing tricks on me, I'm so very tired …

I look back towards the lake.

There is a small, squarish shape sitting on the path, just where it levels out. A dark package, tied with plain string.

I whirl around completely, trying to remain calm, trying to scour the trees without appearing to. What might he be plotting, what kind of ambush? The last sane part of my mind says *leave it be, think on the price you will pay*.

Never you, Rose. Never you.

I dash forward, seizing the parcel as I spin about and race back up the rise, nearly tripping in my haste, cursing my heavy clogs, my thick skirts. Even after I cross back into the noise, I keep running, clasping that solid weight to myself. Not until our gate comes into view do I slow, steadying my breath once more, and look at it. That weight, that shape. Only this time it's wrapped in a still-damp oilcloth, the twine soggy with lake water.

It smells of him.

I hide the parcel in the barn, then go in for supper.

I use the sounds of my parents' snoring to slip outside and run shivering to the barn. Once back in my room I light my candle and tuck it in a corner, shading it behind my bed. Only then do I undo the wrapping.

Not one but two volumes: *Great Queens of Europe*, and *First Latin Primer*.

I thought myself done with tears, but I start crying again. The books are older, but the words are crisp on the page. There are even pictures in *Great Queens of Europe*, pictures of women riding horses, leading armies, standing on balconies before a sea of kneeling subjects.

I knew it the moment I saw you.

Why did no one tell me that a queen could rule?

I spread the books open on my bed, angling them towards the candlelight. The house quiet now, the window shuttered against the cold winds. For a moment I am small again, Tim sprawling beside me, our heads pressed together as we read from the same book. I never knew how happy I was. And if I had known I would lose it all, what might I have done?

I start turning the pages, but I cannot focus on the words. The black marks swim and double. When I move the page close to my face, they straighten into letters but my eyes start to throb, the pain spreading swiftly through my temples.

And you do know this sewing is making you blind?

My stomach heaves. I can feel the scream rising and I jam my fist in my mouth to smother it, howling against my cold knuckles as I have not done since I was small.

At dinnertime Abigail wiggles close to me. She's so bright-eyed she's almost shining, even here in our dingy workroom. "I'm sorry about yesterday," she says.

I shrug, keeping my eyes on my little bowl. What does it matter now? Besides, I have other things to think on: he was not there this morning. Something is changing. I must not let him get the better of me.

"So, who is he?" Abigail whispers loudly in my ear.

"Who is who?" For a moment I cannot think who she means. The only *he* I see on a regular basis is Father. Even Sam Masterson is only a face I greet on Sundays.

"Your fellow. The one you see on the way home."

I stare at her, the food nearly falling out of my gaping mouth. I have never thought of him in any context other than my walk. That he can be seen by the likes of Abigail Fitzwilliam—I have a sudden urge to slap her.

"Ah-ha! There is one!" She claps her hands. "So, who is it? I couldn't see his face. Not from the village … a woodcutter's son?"

"Abigail," I say, in a low growl that seems to come from another Rose.

"Rose, you must tell me, or I shall simply die!" She almost pushes me off the chair, she's leaning in so.

"Abigail, don't."

"I promise I won't tell anyone, not even Sam … if you'll do something for me." She giggles. "I'll keep mum if you introduce me. Today. After all, he might have a brother, all big and strapping, eh?"

I feel it then: something inside me, something new

and hard and cold, as cold as his touch. A shape just starting to form. I cannot see it, but I can feel it, sense it like the blind woman I am becoming.

"Why not?" And for the first time in ages, I smile.

Abigail twitches with impatience. Excitement makes her cheeks flush and she looks almost pretty. That afternoon I had carefully kicked my glove far away, under the hutch that holds the spools of thread, the cushions bristling with small fine needles. Now I stand in mock bewilderment, shaking my head.

"Oh, leave your stupid glove," Abigail says. "You shouldn't keep a boy waiting."

I bite my lip, trying to appear on the verge of tears. "Go on ahead," I say. "Tell him I'm coming. You can walk slowly and I'll catch you up."

She hesitates. "I don't know if I should …"

"Please, Abigail. I don't want to keep him waiting, but Mother will be furious if I lose my glove."

And that's all it takes: she's off, nearly falling down the path in her ardor. Every boy in the village has already been a victim of her fawning interest, and her mother is equally scheming. A new prospect, who might not have heard of her? It's a wonder she lingered as long as she did.

Slowly I gather up my glove and begin walking home, my steps measured, trying to make as little noise as possible. Like it was fated. Every other choice boxed off, until there was only this path, this inevitable moment.

I walk. The sun has nearly set, the last thin band of light like a smudge of fire on the horizon. Overhead the stars are coming out, the rising moon a white sickle. There are the cries of night birds, the higher-pitched whistling of the first bats.

I reach the curve, and the world falls silent.

Does Abigail still hear noises? Or did it fall silent for her as well, only she was so taken with her foolish hope that she just kept barreling towards him?

As I pass the lake I can just glimpse them between the trees, their two dark shapes silhouetted. I slow but I do not stop. Not like Abigail. She is rock-still by the lake's edge, looking up at him. Her coat hangs open, her bare hands resting on his arms.

He is not that tall when he walks with me. Tall and yet somehow on all fours—? My vision doubles, making his dark shape seem to blur and swell.

She puts her leg back, trying to move away, but she cannot. I see now that she is stuck to him, her torso fused against his broadening chest. He rears back, growing in size, and she is pulled along with him as if strapped to him. For a moment they are a towering mass, his dark animal's rearing form and her small body glued to him.

He leaps up and into the water, arcing high in the air and diving in headfirst. Though there is a tremendous spray at their impact, rising up nearly to the tops of the trees, it makes no sound. No water seems to splatter outward, no waves form. The spray merely rises up and vanishes.

The last thing I see are Abigail's small clogs and his dark, elongated feet, the toes rounded and fused together, looking for all the world like hooves.

I walk faster now, my head down as if against a strong wind though there is no wind.

"That's my girl," he whispers in my ear.

I step forward into the long somber cry of an owl, into safety, my heart hammering in my chest.

They find Abigail's body at first light. The knock comes just as I am reaching for my coat, and before Mother can get the door open all the way Bart Masterson is inside, bellowing for Father. In the confusion no one notices when I follow them to the lake. There are several men, filling the silence with their voices, angry and shouting, and between them all the little heap of Abigail's body. She is twisted and bitten, so much so she resembles some animal's carcass, not the girl I knew.

I feel a deep, shuddering wave of pity and regret; my eyes sting with tears, and then it's gone. Before anyone sees me, I hurry back to the house. I've learned all I need to know.

I am kept home that day, and the next. I listen to my

parents arguing, phrases such as *but you said you killed it* and *what about the money she makes?* and I understand. I understand that they are weighing my salary against my life, against the risk of my returning to Mrs. Duggan's.

On the third day they summon me. In winter, to carry us through, Father mends harnesses; he does this now as I sit down, his fingers teasing out worn reins and straps, cutting and fitting the newer leather.

"Sam Masterson has been to your father, Rose," Mother says. "He has asked permission to call on you."

She says this brightly, but there is no joy in her eyes. I simply look at the table.

"He's really taken a fancy to you," Father says. "He says you're the prettiest girl in the village. He's got a good piece of land already in his name, and his father has a finger in every pie in this county. He's one of the wealthiest men around. Look at how they've ridden out this blight: it's barely touched them. You'd be a real help to them too, now that Bart's getting on."

"You'd be taken care of," Mother continues. "You'd be safe from all this. Besides, look at some of the girls in the village, still at home in their twenties. Ask any of them if they'd trade with you, I know they'd say yes. Ask Abigail Fitzwilliam," she adds, her voice tinged with sorrow.

"I thought—" I speak carefully, perhaps for the last time. "I thought perhaps I could go to school again. To become a teacher."

"A teacher?" Father drops the leather. "What the hell gave you that idea?"

"I know you enjoyed school," Mother puts in hurriedly. "But Rose. That's a special thing, becoming a teacher. Those girls come from money, they come from better families. We don't have a penny to spare, what with Tim doing so well." Her smile grows tight. "Or would you have us ruin his chances?"

I bow my head; inside I feel a last door shutting. Only my path now.

"Now Sam's coming here tomorrow, before supper. He's asked to take you for a walk, and then we'll all eat together." She rises. "I expect you to be nice to him, Miss."

Father has already turned back to the harness, but as soon as I shut the door upstairs I hear them again. *Headstrong* and *your fault for letting her go to school so long* and *at least we have Tim.*

They have Tim. And I have myself.

I wait until they're asleep, then I creep on silent, bare feet out into the icy night. Before me, the road to the lake beckons. Soon, soon. Instead I go into the shed, feeling my way until I reach the high hooks where Father keeps the most dangerous tools: the axe, the filleting knife, the skinning knife with the gut hook. I test each one, trying to see them in my mind's eye, their weight and their heft, how easily they can be concealed.

At last I take my chosen weapon and hurry back to bed.

For the first time in years I dream myself in armor.

At close quarters, Sam Masterson is as oafish as he looks from afar, all grinning and hunched shoulders. Thin hair combed at a harsh part, his face and neck washed, but I can see the grime below his collar, under the cuffs of his best shirt. He has brought me a bouquet of pine branches studded with cones.

"You can make a wreath out of them," he offers. "My sisters like to do that."

I thank him and curtsey. I can tell this pleases my parents, I can sense them both relaxing.

He talks about the next year's outlook with Father. From the way he rattles on I know he's parroting Bart's ideas. I meekly set the table with Mother, who beams at me. I've been making a good show of it all day, reading to her from Tim's book and asking her timid questions about running a house, watching as she starts the roast even though I've seen it done a hundred times before.

All this, and I even managed to slip away with my coat for a while, to sew a pouch into the lining of my coat while it's still light. *It needs mending*, I said to her puzzled expression. *I don't want him to think I don't take care of my things.*

Now she goes up to Father and lays a hand on his arm. He clears his throat.

"Perhaps you'd like to take a walk before supper?" he asks.

Sam nods. Only then does he give me a look, like he's sizing me up.

Before we are even past the gate his hands are everywhere, his mouth on mine, thick tongue pushing in. I can't get my breath. Not slow circles like *his* hands, but grasping and pulling like my breasts are teats, then lower, yanking my pelvis against his. In the lining of my coat, the skinning knife jostles against my hip, and I quickly move his hands back up.

He pulls back, his eyes gleaming. "You are a goer, aren't you?" His hands kneading my breasts like dough. "Abigail said you had a fellow, you were going in the woods with him."

I look away, biting my lip. "Poor Abigail," I say.

"It was terrible," he says, as if discussing the weather. "I wouldn't mind, you know, if you had gone with someone for a bit. I like it when a girl knows what to do." He looks back at the house, then pushes me against a tree, grinding his pelvis against mine. "Just a quick one," he says, trying to work my legs apart. "We'll be married soon enough, it's not wrong."

I manage to wiggle free, but just. He's stronger

than I thought. As he grabs me again, his hand trying to get under my coat, I say, "Not here."

That makes him pause. "Oh?"

"There's a place in the woods, by the lake." I frown. "Only Father says I mustn't go there, what with Abigail and all."

"Did you go with one of my mates?" he asks, and there's an edge to his voice now. "I'll bust their heads, I will. Everyone knew I fancied you."

"No, no one you know," I say quickly, trying to think and appear coy at the same time. "Just the one boy, from the far side of the county. And we never did … that. Only other things. I didn't even want to," I add, looking down at my clogs. "Only he wouldn't listen, he made me, I couldn't stop him."

And when I look up at Sam's moonface, my gaze slowly traveling up, over his breeches twisted with his lust—when I look up at his face, I know I have him.

"Show me," he says.

Through the woods and into the silence. I lead Sam by the hand, smiling at him over my shoulder. Every now and then he stops and grabs me, pushing his tongue in my mouth again, groping at my backside. I shudder not in pleasure or disgust, but at the stopping. We need to get far enough that Mother cannot call us back.

We step off the road and onto the damp ground, near the edge of the lake. I tense, waiting for *him* to appear. But there is only the mud sucking at my clogs and Sam Masterson pushing me backwards until I stumble against a log and fall to my knees. At once he's on top of me, pressing me under him. My head scrapes against the log as he kisses me. He weighs so very much, he's pushing all the air from my lungs.

"No," I gasp. "No, wait."

My skirt's up now and he's yanking at my drawers with one hand, squeezing my breast with the other. I try to get away, try to push him off, but my clogs just dig deeper into the soft dirt.

"I knew you'd feel like this," he says. "Touch it nice. You know how."

"No," I say to the sky as he grabs my hand and moves it. Not like this.

Anything but this.

Somewhere in a bright-colored world, Queen Rose steps out on her balcony into the sunlight and her people cheer her name *Rose Rose Rose*.

"Rose," Sam huffs against me, shoving his pants down. "Rose, I can't wait, stop trying to close your legs, damn it."

All I can see is his face leering at me, like I'm someone else, like I'm nothing. He wedges my knees apart, his fingers digging into my flesh.

A greengrey hand, its skin shiny with moisture, wraps across Sam's face and wrenches his head to one side. There is a crack, so loud it makes me scream.

"Rose, Rose, Rose," he chortles. "Lovely Rose, I'm starting to think it's *you* who wants *me*."

He wraps his squelching arms around Sam,

drawing Sam's limp body up against his own. Only then do I feel how my thighs are trembling. It's hard to push myself up onto the log, to turn aside enough to work my drawers back up. And then I keep my body angled away from him, feeling inside my coat until I find the slit in the lining.

When I seize the knife, I start to cry.

The each-uisge is swelling and rising, his body expanding with each breath like a bellows. His elongated head blots out the stars. The Sam stuck to his chest is no longer Sam but some still, glassy thing. I can still taste his spittle. I see that his pants are hanging off his hips, his penis small and flaccid, and I cry harder now.

"Rose," he says thickly, nuzzling Sam's head. "My poor little Rose, I'll just be a moment. Why don't you lie down again, and when I come back I'll make everything much better."

"You said you would free me," I say, my voice quivering.

"And I will, pretty," he coos, taking a step backwards. "I just have to take care of your swain first, and then I'll show you a different way to read."

"You said you would make me a queen," I say again. "*Your* queen."

As he starts to reply I lunge forward, seizing Sam's shirt with my free hand like it was the handle of a shield. My shield. We topple backwards and I swing the cruel curved knife out wide and around, driving it into the softness behind Sam's body, burying it to the hilt in his cold flesh. I can feel him scream but we're already beneath the water, sliding into a strange thick darkness, falling down, down, down.

He trudges along the road, somber in his crisp black suit. As he crosses into my lands he pauses, looking around. I would know him anywhere, even now with his pretentious lace cuffs, the white cravat that would be soiled by the simplest chores.

My brother, the gentleman.

Tim comes to the edge of the lake and looks around again, his eyes gleaming with tears. He bows his head and begins to pray.

For a moment I think to let him pass but his praying irks me, his clothes irk me. As if he were clad in my very tears. Would he even be here, now, would he even have bothered to write, had I become the good Missus Masterson? Like hell he would. Like hell.

I rise up out of my waters. My waters, my lands. My *realm*. As are the books in my library, as are the roads I fashion between my waters, roads that take me through the world. I am practicing languages I did not know existed, I have seen cities unlike anything I ever imagined.

That creatures great and small shun my roads—it is a small price to pay. That I still have a higher power I must bow to, that I must appease from time to time with the sweet, plump essence of three victims—well, it is a far cry from sewing buttonholes, or having to give service to Sam Masterson.

Tim finishes his prayer and raises his eyes to me and screams. I am gratified.

"Rose," he gasps. "Rose, what have you done?"

"Darling, lovely Tim," I say, smiling. "*Flectere si nequeo superos acheronta movebo.*" I take a step forward, and another. I can smell his fear and it is marvelous. "It's Virgil, Tim. 'If I cannot deflect the will of Heaven, I shall move Hell.' Whatever do they teach you in that university of yours?"

"Your eyes," he whispers.

"Whole and well and *mine.* Already they have seen more than you will ever know." I stretch my arms out to him. "Never to be taken from me. Never, Tim. *Vivat Regina.*"

I take him with me into my lake.

WE ARE SIRENS

1.

WE ROLL into town on a bright sunny morning,
steering the Caddy around the half-dozen streets that
make up "downtown:" three of us in the back dozing
and the other two up front with our arms hanging out
the windows, letting our fingers ride on the fall air.

We love autumn. Autumn is football and soccer
and tennis season, it's harvest festivals and Oktober-
fests and the last round of carnivals and fairs. We can
still get away with tank tops and shorts, or we can
wear our tight wool suits with their snug skirts, or our
sweaters with the necklines way, way down.

It just depends on what there is to do around here.

We roll the Caddy into two parking spaces and we
pile out, lounging against the car and sizing up the
people, reading the flyers posted on windows and
utility poles. Free movie nights, a potluck, two
spaghetti feeds, a reading at the library. When we find

the town fair poster we groan in disappointment: it's two weeks away.

"Hey," we call out to a passing kid. "What's there to do around here?"

The kid looks us over, his round little face intrigued and suspicious.

"Big game's tonight, over at the high school," he says, scratching at the back of his calf.

The big game. We sigh with pleasure. We love big games, and their parties afterwards. Big games are easy; we'll be spoiled for choices.

The kid squints at us. "Where're you from?" he asks.

We crouch down to study his rocket ship t-shirt and his cargo pants with bulging pockets, his oversized sneakers, his rosy-cheeked face. These boys, they're a blur to us until their voices break, nothing but sticks and snails and puppy dog's tails. We love them because of what they'll become.

"We're sirens," we say, smiling at him. "We're from everywhere."

Big games mean guys from other towns, with two, maybe three parties afterwards. Big games mean the red suitcase, not the blue or the grey. In the red suit- case we have the high school clothes: the miniskirts and tennis shoes, the t-shirts and the lipstick as red as the cherry slurpees we grab on our way to the field. In the red suitcase we have five denim jackets with patches on the back that say SIRENS, because for the big game we're always an out-of-town gang, tough girls from some generic City that turn heads and make the adults scowl and whisper, make the mothers especially suck their teeth in disapproval and the fathers agree though with a gleam in their eye, a gleam that remembers what it was like to be a teenage boy watching the tough girls and wondering if it was all true, what they said about tough girls.

We take our slurpees and we climb up to the top of the bleachers and sprawl there, our bare legs loose and splayed on the warm metal, the wind ruffling at our skirts. We slurp our slurpees with our pursed red lips and we hum, just loud enough for the wind to hear.

We hum the call of Hades, so he'll be ready for his new arrivals.

And as always, we pause and listen. We used to hear an answering melody, like a shepherd's pipes, or a warbling chorus of birds, or a farmer suddenly bursting into song. But though we strain to hear there is only the rumbling of the crowd and the blaring loudspeaker announcing names.

It's been a long, long time since the gods answered us.

But we are sirens, and we were made to sing.

We settle in to wait as the game kicks off, scratching the bumps of our wings against the railing of the bleachers, our legs tangling pink and olive and brown as we play footsie with each other. We sing in whispers of other sunny days spent waiting, watching games being played, watching carts and horses pass-ing, watching our meadow-grass bending in the wind or the surf crashing against our shore.

We have been this way a long time, and some time, and not long at all, for all times are then and now and everything between. We will be and we have been and we always are, and that's all we need to know.

And damn, but we love us some cherry slurpees. One of us farts and some of us titter and we slurp until our straws are sucking air. The final whistle is like birdsong and we sing in response: *it's time it's time it's time.*

We join the crowd hanging around the school after-ward, nodding to the guys as they pile out of the building, shower-fresh and slapping hands and swag-gering. We love that swagger, we love the dewy hairs on their napes and their still-flushed skin. We sit on the gold-colored hood of the Caddy and poke and kick at each other and we feign boredom while we pick and choose like they're sweets in a shop.

The girls give us side-eye looks and the guys mutter and snigger and we're humming *our* song, our dangling feet kick in time with it, our fingers drum it on the warm metal. When they start to disperse we call out, "So where's the party?"

One guy walks over to us and he's already a man, filled out and stubbly, and we see the girls watching him watching us and our hum changes to a contented trill. Oh, he will do. Oh, he will do us nicely.

"Where you from?" he asks.

"The city," we say with a shrug.

"We're visiting her aunt out here. Got sent to the boondocks to straighten us out."

"It was either that or juvie."

"You guys gotta do something for fun."

"We haven't been to a good party in ages," we finish, to seal the deal.

He looks us over, appraising just as we appraised him, but we titter because we know we're assessing very different things.

"Jason's dad is out of town," he says with a twitch of his head. "We're gonna pick up a couple kegs and go out there tonight."

Two of his friends have sidled up behind him, their pads and helmets dangling from their hands; the setting sun torches their faces so we can see their very skulls.

"So, you're in a gang or something?" one asks, his voice full of fake scorn, as if the thought doesn't make his heart race.

"We're our own gang," we say. "We're the Sirens. And we like to party." We hop off the car, dusting our skirts so the hems flutter around the tops of our thighs. "Give us the address and we'll meet you there."

They confer among themselves and manage to come up with a pen but no paper; we sigh and take off our jacket and hold out a bare arm. The big one, the man, writes the words in rough strokes along the soft inner skin, and while he leans in close we whisper our song in his ear, the one we love best, and he trembles and drops the pen. When he bends to pick it up we spread our legs a little, our skirt brushing against his face as he stands.

"We'll see you there," we say. "What's your name, anyway?"

"Uh, everyone calls me Big Mac," he says, red-faced.

At once we fall about laughing. We haven't laughed this hard in ages. Both a song and a meal! We feel the threads of fate close around us, we sense our meandering path become the purposeful soaring of flight. Still snickering, we hum the first notes: *two all-beef patties* ...

"Of course you are," we say. "We'll see you soon, Big Mac."

When we show up to the party we park the Caddy way down the road and leave our jackets behind, folding them up carefully and putting them back into the red suitcase. We like our jackets too much to risk ruining them and there will be ruining tonight.

Instead we put on cheap t-shirts and our special skintight pants that are as tricky as chastity belts. We do our eyes dark and our lips red. In the dim light of the streetlamp our little mirrors reflect back five bloody-mouthed skulls.

We sing the song of approval, our harmonies spot-on; we sing of long ago lakes and rivers and oceans and our reflections in those waters, hollow-eyed and bloody-mouthed, and how the lapping of the waves was also the rhythm of the gods' approval.

"As if they could keep us trapped in those rocks," we say. "As if."

"Someone has to sing, I don't see anyone else doing it."

"Someone has to test their mettle." The word *mettle* makes us smile like cats.

"It's why Hades made us, after all."

"One Big Mac for Big H, coming up!" We fall about giggling again.

We walk up the drive to the party, our arms filled with bags. We've come prepared: we've got hard liquor and weed and long pretzel sticks we can suck on, we've got our tight pants with their trick openings and our bad-girl smiles, and we're ready to get this party started. Because these parties are never like the movies, there's never shoulder-to-shoulder dancing and making out; instead there's cliques huddled in corners sipping flat beer and smoking pin-thin joints and that just won't do, that won't do at all. We like dancing, we like groping and kissing, we like sweat and lust and nervousness all at once, we like a build-up so that when the time comes, all of that energy gets transmuted into a spine-cracking terror that makes all the humours gush forth and tastes like heaven.

Everything else is just gravy.

Inside we turn that music *up*. We start dancing with ourselves while we sneak off and spike a few bottles of soda in the fridge; we light up and smoke a little and we dance to our rhythm which is the rhythm of pop songs. "You don't get this stuck in a rock," we tell each other, and we sing out our agreement in time with the music. Sure enough, others start dancing with us, we're moving furniture out of the way and there's more smoke in the air and bodies are sliding around us and now we're feeling it, that rush of anticipation. We can see eyes watching us and we can feel bodies moving towards us and we twist and shimmy in time with the music *closer closer closer*.

We are pulled aside by another boy-man who starts dancing close and we sing *yes*.

We are stumbling up the stairs with damp lips on our lips and strong hands on our hips and we open our mouths to theirs and into the beery chasm of their throats we sing *yes*.

Throughout the house our five bodies trill and we whisper, "let's go for a drive and we can really party," and we hum in unison *yes yes yes*.

And we're stumbling through a hallway, around bodies and over bodies and leading the warm sweaty hand in ours, when a door opens and a girl comes out. Her eyes are swollen and she looks like she's going to be sick. She's wearing her jacket and it's buttoned all the way up.

We know about buttoned-up jackets and coming out of bedrooms with eyes swollen from crying.

A guy comes out behind her, looking both sated

and pissed off, and we ignore the one with us and instead sing to him, this Bedroom Boy, we sing to him. For we know about swollen eyes and buttoned-up jackets and we know the sweetness of surf crashing on rock and our song is *Bedroom Boy, are we gonna make you crash*. It's new and old all at once, it's a song we've sung since we can remember and it's a song about this boy, this night, right now.

We offer the girl our drink and she tries to take a sip but then starts heaving and we know about this too. We hum *girl*, we hum *swollen eyes buttoned jacket throwing up*, and our hum fills the house with a mixture of trepidation and delight and we start the crash song all over again.

The girl looks around, wiping at her running eyes. "What's that weird music?"

And then it is like a movie, because the world goes quiet as we study this girl, there's something about her, something we can't put our finger on. When was the last time a girl heard us? Ages ago, we think; ages ago, when we were four and became five, because a girl heard us.

We call out a new chorus: *she hears us*. We listen to the silence, we feel the utter shock through the house, we hear the rhythm of bewilderment. Until at last we call out our response, from five mouths at once: *then she comes with us*.

We're making out in some big van-car with guy-breath and guy-hands while we barrel along some dark road. The girl sits in the far back with us and she's finally started drinking, trading gulps from the bottle and listening to the wet smacking and grunting and our feet tapping in time. We have Bedroom Boy with us and we've promised the girl we're going to do something terrible to him. In response the girl said her name is Sarah, but otherwise she's stayed quiet, a wary expression on her face.

"So, you're like a gang or something?" the Sarah-girl finally asks. Her eyes have stopped running but now she's wiping her nose over and over.

"We're sirens," we agree, taking another long swallow.

"Like the *Odyssey?*"

Odysseus.

Fear makes us convulse in a long body-wrenching shudder that spirals out into the night, following the threads of fate that connect all the sirens we have been and will be, so that everywhere and everywhen we are shuddering, in cities and villages and open plains and rocky coasts, aloft on our black wings or still stuck in the mire of this world singing *yes come to us yes*, we all to a one shudder.

Oh, we have not thought his name in so long.

Turned to rocks, just for doing our *job*. Turned to rocks, when he was supposed to *crash*. Turned to rocks for matching cheat to cheat, for leaving our meadow to make him *listen*.

If there's one thing we learned from that time, it's

that the gods are bastards and never, ever to be trusted.

To suffer so, for one stupid man! All those centuries lost, for their precious Odysseus! As if that pointless punishment wouldn't make us mad for the world, wouldn't propel us back into the world hungrier than ever, wouldn't drive us to scream our song into every corner of the world.

As if.

The car squeals and lurches around a corner and the Sarah-girl looks over her shoulder. "Slow the fuck down!" she exclaims, but we turn up the radio and drown her out and go right back to fondling Big Mac and Bedroom Boy and whoever their friend is. He's too bland to inspire a nickname.

"We're going to die," Sarah-girl says. She says it like she doesn't really care. Her eyes are filling again. "What kind of girl," she asks in a shakier voice, "what kind of girl gets in a car with a guy after he treats her like shit? Not a very good one, huh?"

"A girl who wants to see him crash," we say with a grin. "We are sirens, after all."

"The way Mac's driving, we're all gonna crash," she says, and takes another drink. "So why aren't you with someone?"

"Oh, we've got all we need," we say. "We could even lose the boring one, he's just gravy."

She frowns at this. "What's with the we shit? Is it like the royal we?"

The question makes us go quiet again. First a reminder of *him*, now this question. We pause in our groping and lean in close, because this is very serious. "There is only we," we explain. "We are one and all, we are in time and not, we are past and present and future. We are sirens." We lay our hands lightly upon her, wondering at that strange feeling she exudes: of something becoming, something about to burst free. "No you, no I. No doubts or differences. No family save ourselves. Only we, together, singing."

"Yeah, sure. Pick on Sarah, I get it." Her lower lip trembles. "You know that's a stereotype, right? I don't have a shitty family and I don't need your weird hive-mind clique." She takes the bottle from us and drains it. "You can all go fuck yourselves."

Her every word thrills us. We look at her and we see ourselves as we were before becoming this: that unknown longing, that sense of our self being an ill-fitting suit, until at last we heard our song.

How cute she would look with lovely raven-black wings, clawed at the tips, feathers stained with blood!

And then we feel it, and we nod at each other across the car. It's time.

We sing. We sing the song of offering and the guys snigger and call us wannabe rock stars and we sing harder, so hard we drown out the radio. We sing *our* song, the song of *come and get it*, the song of *you know you want it*, the song of crashing against rocks and falling headfirst into waves of grass and groping us in dark van-cars, all because they're hearing the song they've longed for.

The van-car jerks left, shooting off the road and barreling into something hard with a sound as loud as an explosion. We reprise the song of offering, as beautiful as always. More explosions and the guys are screaming in time with our song, the car hurtles into empty space in time with our song. We seize Sarah-girl and burst through the glass, unfurling our wings as the car falls away below us and crashes against the rocky hillside, shattering and bouncing and then finally landing in a steaming heap below.

In our arms Sarah-girl screams and screams, clinging to us with a good amount of strength. All things we like in a girl: this death-grip and her lusty wailing. We spiral downwards like the mighty vultures we are, our song that of flesh and appetite and the underworld. Deep and rich, this song, it comes from our bellies and makes our thighs tremble. Sarah-girl too goes quiet, and we croon our thanks and settle on the ground at last. When we let her go she curls her knees to her chest and starts rocking back and forth. And though we say nothing we hum to each other *the rocking remember* for we all rocked so in our time, just as we screamed the first time we tasted sky-air, just as we gagged the first time we bit into raw flesh.

All so long ago as to be a story. Besides, we turned out fine.

We toss aside the remains of our t-shirts and bras and stretch our wings to the cool night air. We take a moment to pin back our hair, straight and curly, thin and thick, and then we set to work. We drag the bodies out of the wreck, one after another, bloodied boy-limbs contorted and folded, heads at odd angles and bones jutting from flesh. One's still moaning and we start with him, falling upon him with clawed hands and hungry mouths and when he stops moaning we hear another sound, a rhythmic keening that we rather like, and we all look at Sarah-girl who stops both rocking and keening as our five faces turn to her and her eyes roll up and she falls over in a faint.

We cradle her between us, this Sarah-girl, and we take a mouthful of Bedroom Boy and we chew it into a soft pap and then we kiss our sleeping Sarah-girl, easing his warm soft flesh into her mouth, and we stroke her throat and we sing the song of becoming until, with a jerk, she gulps it down.

We coast on the wind until we're circling the Caddy, loving the starlight and the lights below. How many starlit nights have we flown so? Over mountains and beaches, pitch-black villages and cities like a million scattered jewels gleaming. Gone are the days when we can safely soar in sunlight, and we croon a soft song of regret and time before slowly returning to earth. Our wings disappear, becoming ridges beneath our flesh once more. We can hear music still drifting down from the house. As we drive away into the purpling dawn, our sleeping Sarah-girl sprawls atop our laps in the back seat. She stirs and whimpers baby-like and we stroke her thick black hair and we rub her narrow back but we feel nothing.

Why are there no bumps forming?

We look at each other, trying to remember how it was for each of us: first the feeding of pap, then the wings, then slowly the loss of *I* and the sweet emergence into the warm mind-nest of *us*. How long did it take? We cannot remember, but it doesn't *feel* long, it doesn't feel like it took long at all.

Confused, we peer at her more closely, our hands exploring. Only then do we realize that her breasts are padding; only then do we feel what lies between her legs; only then do we realize what lies nascent in our Sarah-girl is not any likeness to us but the rising question of who she really is, for our Sarah-girl is very much a boy.

We drive and we drive, all night and all day, pulling over only to piss and switch seats. We drive as if something were following us, as if we were being chased to the very ends of the earth. Or at least across state lines.

We cannot sleep. We slouch, silent and pale, watching and not watching Sarah-girl in her uneasy slumber between us, her head rolling and flopping as the Caddy sways. We whisper to each other, "the gods didn't send her, it's just coincidence, she'll change or crash anytime now," but we do not believe our own words.

When she awakens, she only glares at each of us, then turns and watches the unfolding landscape, as tense and as silent as we are.

And though we dare not admit it, we are, each of us, flexing elbows and knees for any hint of stiffness. We turn our palms this way and that way, we slide our feet in and out of our shoes thinking to glimpse any hint of cold greying. For that's how it came upon us last time, sneaking in like a chill, creeping through our bodies until we realized we could neither run nor fly nor even touch one another, not even just to give a last brief comfort …

Watching Molpe's face vanish in a wall of stone, and I could not even say her name …

The Caddy lurches as we steady ourselves. But it cannot be unthought. That *I*-shaped crack in our defenses.

We make our hands into fists and keep driving.

Until at last it ends, as everything does, for we're running out of gas.

2.

In this town it's convention time: the streetlights are festooned with banners proclaiming it, the bus stops have posters proclaiming it, there are lunch specials for convention-goers and vacancies for convention-goers and cheap parking for convention-goers.

There's a snap in the air and a river running right past the hotel, and there are lovely balconies with flimsy railings and blind curves of traffic and pathways that veer close to the jutting rocks of the riverbed. We look at the river and we hum *remember*, for we long to be back where the grasses wave in the breeze and the sea sits glass-smooth and empty. We touch each other and softly sing how it used to be, in the cool grasses beneath the warm sun, our wings drying and our bodies drowsy, singing simply to hear our voices in the world.

How it was before Odysseus.

We should be opening the grey suitcase which contains our wool skirts and silk blouses, we should be combing our hair smooth and pinning it in such a way that it can tumble free the moment the pin is withdrawn. Instead we're standing around the Caddy in a deserted parking lot because Sarah-girl is huddled half-in and half-out of the backseat and we're afraid to touch her, even as we long both to hug her and break her neck.

Sarah-girl says, "He didn't deserve that." She has said this many times since we pulled off the road. It's a song we know, the one of guilt and remorse, but we never sing it because it has no end.

She says, "Okay, yes, he was a homophobic asshole, but I mean, in a way I kinda led him on, and you can't just kill people for being homophobic assholes. Right?"

We shrug. When she looks at us expectantly we say, "It doesn't matter what he was, Sarah-girl."

"Some hear the song and crash, and some don't. Swings and roundabouts."

"Sometimes they're nice, sometimes they're assholes."

"What is constant is that we sing, Sarah-girl. Someone has to sing—"

"So, this is what you do?" She bursts in before we can continue. "I thought you were, like, temptresses or something. You keep saying you just sing, but you're acting like serial killers."

"But that's the *song*," we snap at her. It's all we can do to keep from shaking her, why won't she understand? She heard us and she's still alive and she's not changing; either the gods are fucking with us or we've missed something, something terribly important. What does it matter what we are?

We are sirens. As we have always been.

We realize then that she's cringing, maybe even about to scream, so we take a deep breath and say more calmly, "It's the song we sing, Sarah-girl. We sing to those who want to hear, whose fates lead them to us."

"You sing to men," she says in a smaller, trembling voice.

We shrug again. "Mostly. Women crash in other ways."

"And I heard you," she says in her smaller voice. "And I, I was—"

"We know," we say, in perfect chorus.

"Are you going to kill me, then?"

The vision fills us at once: piling into the car and

pinning her while she screams and cries. Breaking her neck, one swift wrench and then the sudden silence. Her body in the trunk, the suitcases piled in her place on the backseat. A swift tumble in the river at nightfall. And if we did it all, if we killed her and threw her body in the water and drove away, only to feel our limbs grow heavy, our own bodies smothering us?

"We're only supposed to sing, Sarah-girl," we say again, but we can hear the quaver in our voices.

She wrenches her jacket more tightly about herself and we find ourselves mimicking her, wrapping our arms around ourselves, unable to look anywhere but at her. "So, I've heard you, and I'm alive, and I haven't turned into some winged murderess," she says. "So then I'm nothing, right? Not one thing or the other. So I can, just, go home?"

We only look at her.

"But didn't you let Odysseus go? I mean, he survived …"

But her voice grows smaller as she speaks, she can see our anger, and at the *survived* she starts to cry. We hate her now, we hate her tears and her smallness that reminds us of when we were *I*, we hate her for reminding us of *him*, we hate her for going to that party like an idiot, what was she thinking? As if they wouldn't see her as something to bully and abuse, as if the world has changed that much.

As if.

"Homer never sang what happened to *us*, Sarahgirl," we say coolly.

"He never cared about any of us. Only Odysseus,

Odysseus, great-hearted Odysseus." We sing the name out in a whining screech.

"He didn't even bother to *count*. There were more than two of us that day, we can tell you that."

"Precious cunning Odysseus who made us fail for a *joke*, for his own *cleverness.*"

"We tried to play our own joke. We tried to bite off his stopped-up ears." We snap our teeth in the air, imagining the blood of Odysseus on our tongues, how his cartilage would crack and pop like chewing gum. "Do you know what happens when you attack the gods' favorite city-sacker? When even Hades turns his back on you?"

We crowd around her now, our shoulders itching, our wings straining at our shirts and our hands balling into fists. "We're never going back!" we yell at her. "Do you understand? We are *never* being changed again!"

"Please don't!" Sarah-girl cries out, throwing her arms over her face. "Please, I don't want to die!"

Her voice brings us up short, as swift and sure as if she struck us. For those were our words, then, our single voices jangling as we fell, our limbs stiffening and our bodies suddenly so cold. *I don't want to die!* Our tears streaming down our faces, our song thin and weak from our closing throats:

All that I had left undone,
All that I wanted,
All that I hoped,
All that I longed for,
All that I was, I don't want to die!

Our body-prisons, our caged minds and their lonely calling: blindly we fling our arms out, each feeling for the other, even as we come back together in a rush of awareness that leaves us breathless.

In the back seat of the Caddy, Sarah-girl is still crying, oblivious to everything but her own fear. Weren't there other Sarah-girls before? Women's souls in men's bodies, men's souls in women's bodies, all the children of Hermaphroditus and those who claimed no sex at all. What song did we sing to them, what did they do? If we let ourselves remember, if we could just remember before *him*—

But all we remember is that cold, lonely oblivion, and how we finally freed ourselves by singing our song which is all the songs of crashing, fast and slow, sweet and cruel. For that was then and this is now and between then and now is rock, and we are going back for no one, not even Sarah-girl. Yet when we start to hum, it feels wrong, it feels like we're singing to ourselves.

Instead, we do the only thing we can think to do.

"Damn it all," we say. "We need a drink."

We dress from the grey suitcase, silent and grim, scraping our hair back and twisting it violently, gouging our lips into pencil-sharp bows begging to be undone. We turn our attention to Sarah-girl then, managing to prise her out of her jacket and into a cardigan, though she keeps clutching the jacket to herself.

"You're our intern," we tell her, and for once she simply nods.

We go to the convention, but in truth we don't care, we don't care about the men in their off-the-rack suits with their little name cards clipped to their jackets and their identical folders tossed about. We barely notice them drinking their beers and liquors, we wince at the din of their bellowing voices, and we go up to the bar as silent as if we're already lost.

"Six Cosmo—"

But before we can complete the phrase, we start babbling other names.

"Gimlet."

"Lemondrop."

"Glass of cabernet."

As we speak, our minds flicker in and out, buffeting each other with moments of dark loneliness before we are one again, and we cannot meet each other's eyes.

"Martini."

With a sigh, we add, "*One* Cosmopolitan."

"Water."

At the last we all look at each other, astonished, until we realize it was Sarah-girl speaking. She frowns at the bar. "What? I'm underage."

We elbow her and step on her foot. "You're our intern," we whisper loudly. "You can't be underage."

"I can be whatever I want to be," she retorts.

"Get her a Cosmopolitan," we say to the bartender, only to shake our heads.

"Maybe she should choose," we say.

"She'd be better off with a beer."

"She'd be better off with a Shirley Temple."

"We could get her a coke in a little glass, like it's a rum and coke—"

"I want water," Sarah-girl interrupts and we grumble in irritation. "You don't have to do everything alike, you know. Do you all even like Cosmopolitans?"

Our confusion and sorrow suddenly looms large before us, even amidst the bustle and noise of the bar. One by one our drinks appear, so many shimmering colors and shapes, and do we all even like Cosmopolitans? We cannot say—we dare not say, lest we fall apart, lest our differing selves make us vulnerable again. Yet we have not heard a response since we reawakened; we've sung to Sarah-girl and fed Sarah-girl and still she remains herself. Is it that simple, can we just choose what we are?

But we chose once before, and paid dearly for it.

We are *sirens*.

We take our drinks and knock them back and smile gamely. Around us the men are looking, looking and we make ourselves return their gazes, make ourselves run our fingers around the rims of our sweating glasses and steal cherries that we bite free of their stems, feeling the sickly-sweet syrup fill our mouths, tasting for all the world like the blood of a day-old corpse.

"Let's get to work," we say.

These men.

They wear cheap suits and polyester-blend ties that just-so-slightly clash, they smile at us with whitened teeth, they comb their hair over the first patches of bare skin and give themselves little bangs to hide the creep of their hairline. They drink beer and scotch and whiskey and the younger ones do shots.

The convention has something to do with leadership and millennia and these things bore us so we hunker down into a shoal of couches and wait, drinking, hoping against hope that Sarah-girl will start to change or keel over dead and end all our doubt and misery. But she only sips at her water with a big straw, her eyes darting around the room like a cornered rabbit.

"She's our intern," we tell the men when they ask about her. We hold out business cards. "Siren Enterprises. We're human resources."

The words are like code. It's just enough of an excuse; they plop down on our couches and we manage a half-hearted hum while they chatter on about their companies and their roles, their workloads and their successes. All encoded like the songs of birds. Only we cannot help wondering, now: does any of this matter? If we weren't here, would they find other ways to crash?

Through the birdshit-spattered windows we can see the sun setting. We can sense the crowd becoming drunker, sense fates sliding and intertwining—or are we imagining it all?

But we need to begin, if we're going to do this.

There are four men perched on our couches, their long arms extended behind us, and our empty glasses are crowded on the table. A fifth hovers nearby, his head turning at every laugh, eager for an excuse to join us. The piped-in music has gone from light jazz to something more brisk, reminding us of earlier bars and filtered sunlight and hands that want to stroke our knees but aren't yet emboldened. We're wearing our stockings as strong and dense as spiderwebs. our wool skirts tailored tight, and our silk blouses open one button too many for decency.

We try to sing, we try to find the rhythm of this offering, and we're just humming the first harmonious notes when Sarah-girl suddenly giggles. Loudly. One of the men whispers in her ear again and she bursts into a braying, snorting laugh that makes heads turn.

As fractured as we are, as faltering as we are, to a one we narrow our eyes and mutter in unison, "If she changes, we're going to have to work on that."

As if sensing our irritation, one of the men says, "How about we take this party elsewhere? Friend of mine has a suite upstairs, he said to bring anyone looking for a good time."

We feel it then, we feel it at last, that sense of fates coalescing, of wind in the grass and the crashing of waves, and we smile and sing out in unison *good time good time good time.*

In the elevator the music is a tinny samba and we find ourselves singing a song of hot sun and sand and glassy-smooth sea. The men smirk and one tells us, "You girls should start a band" and from behind us Sarah-girl mutters, "oh *please*." Another guy whispers to his friend, "What else can they do with their mouths, huh?" and now it's our turn to smirk because he's about to find out. But before we can sing to Mister Curiosity Sarah-girl says, "You are *so* the gravy, pal," and despite all our fear and misgivings we love her for that.

The music coming out of the television is all thumping synthesizers and the liquor bottles are heavy in our hands and the cocaine up our noses burns like the rising sun. The men stumble against us, laughing. They're pulling off their ties and whispering bad words in our ears as they try to dance to our rhythm which is the rhythm of late night grooves. We sing along with the mimed images on the screen, dark syrupy words about grinding and riding and whipping and shackles and thighs and wet wet lips.

The men push our skirts up and bury their snotty noses in our cleavage and if they weren't so drunk we'd do something about that, we're wearing silk after all. But they are very, very drunk and it's almost time. We sway and watch and sing out *crash baby crash uh huh*. When the first one stumbles to the balcony doors and flings them open we sing *mmmm let's do it* and when two start yelling at each other we sing *hit it sugar* and soon they're rolling and punching and the wind gusts in and our shoulders itch with anticipation and we sing out to Hades *she wants it, she wants it all to crash—*

—and then we realize we cannot see Sarah-girl.

We wedged the hallway door shut when we came in, because no one is leaving this party, and it's still wedged shut so she cannot have gone far. *Come and jump on it, yeah*. We check under the bed, humming *uh-huh uh-huh*: no Sarah-girl. We check the closet *don't stop get it get it*, we check the balcony *I got it goin' on*, and then we seize the handle of the bathroom door and sigh for it will not move. We egg on the fight and we grind against a man on the balcony and we crouch by the bathroom door and whisper, "Sarah-girl."

"I'm not coming out," she says from the other side. "There's a phone in here, and if you try anything I'm going to call for help."

We glance at each other, at our loose hair and our red-smeared mouths and our blouses that we're unbuttoning to let our wings unfurl. "We can't kill you, Sarah-girl. You must change or crash—"

"I don't want to fucking change or crash!" she yells. "I want to leave!" She takes a heaving breath and we know she's crying again. "I thought you were helping me, I thought you were on my side. Everyone talks about sirens like they're cool, like they're these sexy, badass women. But you're all just psychopaths."

"We only sing——" we begin again, irritated.

"So you say," she bursts in. "So why am I here? Not because of some stupid *rules*, not because someone's making you do this. I'm here because you're all *batshit*, you've all lost the fucking plot." Her voice is rising, drowning out the men and the music alike. "Fuck your song and fuck your change! Who died and made you gods?"

On the last her voice changes and it's both her and someone else, a voice we know from long ago, but before we can think it through a man seizes our arm and jerks us upright, his face a snarl as he tries to kiss us and we sing out *crash* but we've messed up, we lost our focus and we messed up. The men swarm around us grabbing and groping, crushing liquor-sticky mouths to ours and trying to wrestle us onto the beds and we remember this, their hands like iron and their weight and their hot stinking breath on our skin

and then we feel nothing but our anger, pure and cold and vast as the night sky

our wings erupt from our backs and we whip the first man off the balcony, sending him sailing into the night with an echoing howl

rattling the bathroom door singing *Sarah-girl come out come out* but it's jumbling with the song of *crash* and our harmonies are jangling and sharp and we drive the next man into the mirror *crash* lamp cord strangling the third man we bite and wrench him *crash*

there's one screaming between the beds and they're everywhere like rats stomp them out *crash*

with a cry we throw our weight against the bathroom door feel the flimsy lock snap and tumble inside

Mister Curiosity goes over the balcony good-bye gravy

thump-thump-thump from the hallway door and *wump-thu-wump* goes the television and Sarah-girl is calling *I'm here, I'm here* with the hallway cries and our singing *crash* and it's all messed up we messed up

and suddenly Sarah-girl sings.

She opens her mouth wide and sings a song we've never heard before, a song of light and dark, of both crashing and flying; she sings of sunlight on deathbeds and regrets cast aside and hands that hold yours in that last coldest hour, and from all sides there is *song*, they *hear* her, there are radios and car stereos and a drunken singalong and a thousand voices belting out an anthem across town

and we're just sirens and somewhere it all went wrong.

The hall door shudders on its hinges and then my mind becomes pin-small, dark and jumbled with memories, and as the door gives way I stumble blindly onto the balcony and out into the air, my wings barely catching the current as I drag myself skyward. So many memories, all the Aglaopes I have been, so many night skies and blood-tinged breezes and oh! I am so small! So meaningless! Around me the others are flapping, struggling to stay aloft, and though we look at each other there is no more *we*, there is only *I* and *you* and *you* and *you* and *you*

and I remember now how I found Raidne annoying and Thelxiope stuck-up, how I desired Molpe but dared not touch her, how I admired Leucosia's wit but envied her closeness with Molpe

and my wings ache, they feel heavy and stiff, and when I hold my palms up to the moonlight the skin is grey and firm, and as I begin to fall I watch the moon recede from me, the very moon is turning away from us. Great hands of earth rise to seize us, fingers of stone closing over us, and the last thing I glimpse is Sarah-girl peering down at us from the balcony with gossamer pale wings unfolding and I say *never again* but I cannot

3.

In my stony cocoon I dream of Sarah-girl, grown tall and broad and so, so strong, striding through her life without fear, her song a song of reckoning without judgment, her winged shadow sheltering all she chooses to love. I dream of her red lips and her death-hooded eyes and those strange pale wings, and as I dream, my tears dry upon my cheeks and my fists tighten.

We are sirens.

And perhaps Sarah-girl was nothing but a test, or perhaps she is what we were meant to be; but we will be and we have been and we always are, and we have a bone to pick with the gods and their spoiled favorites.

Do they really think these rocks can hold us? Oh, they can cage Aglaope and Molpe and Leucosia and Raidne and Thelxiope. But we have been *we* for a long time now, and we haven't forgotten how we made the very stone about us vibrate, how we hummed and trilled and moaned and slowly coaxed from our prison walls a shuddering not unlike a song.

We're sirens, after all. We *sing*.

And when we finally free ourselves, when we finally shatter the rock around us and feel our mind once more as vast as the sky, when at last we stretch our wings and raise our fists and bare our teeth at Hades and his cheating ilk—

—then? We are coming for the world itself. And we are going to make it *crash*.

A HARVEST FIT FOR MONSTERS

ALENE SWUNG the axe up and down, cursing her tiring arms. The blade slid a little further into the upright log. Sweat ran into her eyes and made her armpits slick. She could have gone to town to arrange for some kind of firewood—a day's walking, but easier than the axe. Instinctively, though, she knew that the day she could no longer cut her own wood would be a turning point, from which there was no coming back.

Besides, there was hardly anyone in town now; hardly anyone anywhere. It was a country of old women and little children. All their strength and vigor was rotting in the fields, in the swaths of land lapping at that single contested border, just a line on the maps of madmen.

Or so she thought when she reflected on her circumstances, which she hardly did anymore. She had buried self-reflection with her husband and children, along with a myriad of emotions: happiness, kindness, that particular sorrow that cleanses the spirit. Her husband had been mortally wounded in the volunteer corps of those too old to serve and too inflamed to know better; her daughter had fallen in the fields not five miles from where Alene stood; her son had been killed in a camp accident that she knew was no accident. Once she heard the news of her son's death she had waited for them to come for her, because of the things he had described in his letter. She had even put her house in order, packed a suitcase, chosen a dress to wear for her execution. But the only thing that had arrived was his battered trunk, appearing on her doorstep one morning like discarded refuse, and that had only angered her more: that the terrible things her son had described mattered so little, in the end it wasn't even worth the effort to kill her.

Until now.

She let the axe slip to the ground as she watched the figure walk towards her, erect and purposeful, the grey of his uniform stark against the brown fields. Only the one, though, and on foot. She waited long enough for any vehicles to appear, and then relaxed a little. It still happened from time to time that a soldier would pass through, searching for a way back to the world they remembered. So many landmarks had been razed, they were often stunned as she gently placed them: yes, these were the outskirts of town; yes, this road was the market road; yes, there used to be four great windmills.

Years ago, the windmills; years of war inbetween, and nearly a year of peace now; and still they came. Alene caught up the axe and walked back to the house, wiping her hands on her shirttails. They would want water, and perhaps supper.

At first he was just a shadow in the doorway, made looming and shapeless by the cloth rucksack he carried. She beckoned him inside, the glass of water in her hand. He stepped into the filtered sunlight and the glass fell, shattering between them.

"I'm not him," he gasped, holding up his hands. "I swear! I'm not him!"

Still Alene could not speak for gaping at him, her heart hammering in her chest. A face she had seen only in grainy print, now suddenly alive before her. The General; *her son's* general. The papers had called him Savior, then Butcher. Her son had called him *the Monster—*

"I'm a cousin, nothing more! Just a distant cousin," the man cried, cringing much as she was. "I had nothing to do with him, I curse the day he was born! Please believe me. I have papers, I can prove it, you must believe me. I was merely a soldier, I had no part in his crimes. Please." He took a step backwards. "I just want to go home," he said in a smaller voice.

She felt behind herself, gripped the back of a chair to keep upright. Trying to understand. They had never found him. They had believed him killed in the last, terrible push to reclaim the capital. A cousin? She tried to superimpose the news photos atop the face before her. Certainly he was more gaunt, older. But so was everyone.

"I'll go," he said. "I don't wish to upset you." He managed a lopsided smile. "This accursed face," he added.

"Wait." She shook herself. "Show me your papers."

He hesitated, wary, then reached carefully into his breast pocket and drew forth a worn booklet. He had to extend his arm fully to reach her, the papers pinched in his trembling fingertips. She took them with a decisive flick of her wrist that made him flinch. Now that the shock had worn off, she could think more clearly. How could he have made it so far, if he was the monster? Ever since the treaty was signed they had scrutinized everyone, searching for the last of his conspirators. Impossible that he should have come so far, to find himself on her doorstep of all places, as abandoned as her son's trunk had been.

The name was different; the photo showed a healthier version of the man before her, one that looked nothing like her recollection of the Monster. She had seen many false papers over the years. These looked official.

"You must be thirsty," she said, handing the booklet back to him and gesturing to her little table. "I've had enough mistrust for this life. Haven't you?"

At that his shoulders sagged. "More than

enough," he agreed. With an odd little bow, he crossed the room to the table, sitting down with a sigh and letting his rucksack slide to the floor. The shape of him, how he nearly banged into things, it reminded her of her children's friends, awkward in their adult bodies even as they prepared to fight adult battles. Her throat closed for a moment, though she had thought herself done with crying over the past.

"Thank you," he said, and again when she set a fresh glass before him: "Thank you."

With a nod she set about sweeping up, watching him surreptitiously as she tidied the mess away. He swallowed thirstily, his stubbled throat flexing. A large, ugly scar knotted the tissue beneath his left earlobe, running down his neck to disappear under his collar. A close call. She had seen worse, but she could well imagine the fear and pain from coming so close to dying.

"You have family nearby?" she asked.

"An old friend." He wiped his mouth on his sleeve, then flushed. "I apologize, my manners ..."

"You've had more important things to worry about." But she laid a napkin before him and refilled his glass, then put the last of her loaf before him as well. He tore into it voraciously. Just another man; it could easily have been her son or husband before her.

"I didn't think there was grain, still," he said around mouthfuls.

"Very little." She sat across from him. "Everything is poisoned, but they don't know why. Some say it's chemicals, some say it's all the metal in the ground ...

but I think it's the blood." At his startled look she gestured to the window. "A battle was waged here. We buried so many, we were shoveling for days, and all that blood went into the dirt and isn't that a kind of poison? So much slaughter?" She heard her own voice, loud and shrill, and held up a hand. "I'm sorry. I've been alone too long."

He had paused in his eating. "It must be hard," he said. "To do everything by yourself, at your age."

"We've all learned to do," she replied. "Those of us that are left."

He was nodding even as he pushed more of her bread into his mouth. Still her gaze kept returning to his scar. There was something about it, something that tugged at her, but for the life of her she could not remember what.

He went to rest, though he kept insisting he would be on his way by sundown, and no matter what he would repay her for her kindness as soon as he reached his friend's farm. Despite his exhaustion, it was some time before she heard the creak of the narrow bedframe, and she could not shake the sense that he, too, was listening to her movements—

Oh, she had been alone too long.

She should have been starting their supper, should have been carving up her precious store of root vegetables and scouring the landscape for any last hints of green. Instead she found herself sitting on the bench at the back of the house, where she used to pluck fowl and clean vegetables. The scar bothered her. Why did it bother her? There was something about it ...

Alene had learned, in the last few years, that when she needed to think of something the trick was to think of something else, so she turned over in her mind the old problem of how to grow vegetables again. A raised bed, with some kind of barrier beneath? How small could it be and still sustain her? Who might have good soil that perhaps she could barter for, she still had a little gold—

—and then she thought of her son's letter.

The box had once contained her prayer book, a useless tome, for what had their prayers brought them save death? Only when Alene received the letter had she understood what prayer really was: the decision-making of the choiceless. A last pretense that you had any power in a mad world.

Slowly, reverently, she lifted the lid on the box and laid it aside, letting her fingers brush the yellowed papers within. Five dense, bristling pages. More than he had written in his life, she knew, for had she not taught him his letters? Leaning over him at the table, watching him struggle to trace the words she had painstakingly written over and over.

Five pages that she kept in the box, the prayer book discarded long ago. Kept carefully flat and sealed away, for after the third reading she had felt something change in herself, as if the words had somehow written themselves into her very blood. All her boy's pain, all that he had done, first blindly, then with a terrible understanding. All the suffering caused for one man's madness.

She took the letter out and scanned it, phrases echoing with memory:

> *he told us to cut out their tongues lest they report us*
> *afterwards I found her corpse and the basket only held*
> *a doll*
> *gutting them would be the only message they understood*
> *told me I had to or he would kill her and her sister both*

Until at last she found what she was looking for.

> *Last night he had a woman brought to us. He said she*
> *was a traitor and we had to know what she told them.*
> *She was barely grown. He brought out his tools and*
> *she started screaming ... I tried to reason with him but*
> *he turned on me and the others seized me, and he said*
> *that even if the girl was innocent she could serve his*
> *purpose. She must have seized the knife while he spoke*
> *to me. When he turned back to her she tried to cut his*
> *throat, but though she caught him under the ear she*
> *could not finish the blow ... oh Mother, when they*
> *were done with her you could not tell her from a butch-*
> *er's scraps, and all I could do was* watch—

> *Please understand that this is why I must stop him no*

matter the price. So many already mimic his behavior
and speak his words. I must stop him before he makes
Monsters of us all.

Alene read it through twice before putting it away.
The scarring beneath his ear—oh, it was too similar
to be coincidence. Not the clean line of a knife
wound, but wouldn't he go to great lengths to mask
such a distinguishing mark?

The house answered her with silence. She
thought, *I should kill him now*; she thought, *I must be*
sure.

And then she went outside once more, catching up
her shovel as she strode out into the fields.

He came into the main room just as she was dusting
the pot with a last precious pinch of spice. Though he
rubbed his face as if newly awakened, his uniform
was barely wrinkled. "That smells magnificent," he
said.

She made herself smile at him. "It's merely bone
broth, but it will nourish."

Carefully she ladled out the steaming liquid,
making sure to catch the small pieces of bone, the
slivers of parsnips and onions. When she put his bowl
before him, he nearly dove in, his eyes focused on the
steaming surface. She took her time filling her own
bowl, took her time crossing the room, her every
gesture that of a tired old woman.

At last she sat in her chair and said, "You don't have to wait for me."

For a time there was only the sound of his enthusiastic slurping, the vigor with which he sucked at the bones, piling them beside his bowl. She made as if to sip her own, watching him until he became aware of her scrutiny.

"You're not hungry?" he asked, his expression changing to wariness again.

"I have little appetite at my age," she demurred, but his unease persisted. She made herself take a mouthful and visibly swallow. She had vowed never again, and never again after that, but there had been so little for so long …

before he makes Monsters of us all

He relaxed as he watched her drink, and leaned back with a contented sigh. "That is the best soup I've had in some time," he said. "Could I possibly lure you to my friend's house? He's a good man, not much younger than you."

"I had a husband," she replied. "I don't want another."

"Children?"

"A son and daughter, both lost to the war."

He looked truly abashed, and her resolve wavered. "My apologies. That was thoughtless of me … it's just, sitting here feels so normal, as if nothing has happened."

"Some of us will never have such moments." She raised the bowl to her mouth, pretending to drink again.

this is why I must stop him no matter the price

"Well, we know who's to blame, eh?" He smiled at her. "But we showed them who is the greater. They'll never dare to assault us again."

"I'm not sure there's anyone left to assault us." She rose and carried the bowls to the sink. "You enjoyed the broth?"

"As I said, one of the tastiest meals I've had in many days. Clever of you to keep the bones of your game." Was there a sly tone creeping into his voice? "Another thing you learned to do, or country wisdom?"

"There hasn't been game here in years." She stared into the sink, where the axe lay, and beside it the bullets she had removed from the pistol in his rucksack.

"From a butcher? I'm honored, it must have cost a fortune—"

"I was standing here when it started." She watched his reflection in the window glass, coiling and uncoiling her fingers around the axe handle. "The grain was waist high, it looked like they were floating in it. Thousands of soldiers, so dirty and ragged you could barely tell ours from theirs. They had run out of ammunition. It was knives, swords, even rocks. It was the most brutal sight I had ever beheld."

His reflection shrugged. "It's been terrible, especially this last year. But war is always terrible. We must put the past behind us now and focus on rebuilding."

"I learned my daughter was among them, somewhere, and I took an axe and ran out to find her." She realized she had stopped speaking to him. Who was she speaking to? "It's easy to kill when you can't really see them, when they're just blurs, howling like animals. That was the first thing I learned to do, General. Perhaps you of all people can appreciate such a lesson?"

He straightened in his chair. "I told you, I'm not him." His hands suddenly hidden.

"Afterwards, there was nothing in the field but bodies. I told myself I would starve before I touched them, yet you cannot make a broth without bones." She laughed softly. "No more grain, no more animals, but we have plenty of bones, General. A harvest fit for Monsters."

The click of the pistol made her look over her shoulder. "I think we've had a misunderstanding," he said, taking steady aim at her. "You have been alone too long, grandmother. I am going to leave now. Please don't make me use this."

"Is that what you tell yourself about the girl who cut you?" Alene touched the flesh below her own ear, mirroring his scarring. "It was a misunderstanding? What about the soldiers you ordered gutted after their surrender? The children you swore were carrying ammunition to the front line? My son was one of your lieutenants, General, and he told me *everything*."

He squeezed the trigger but there was only an empty click. Cursing, he lurched to his feet and reached for his rucksack. Alene turned completely, swinging the axe out and wide, crossing the room as fast as she could. She felt strong, as strong as she had in the fields that night, she could already feel the blade driving into his flesh—

stop him before

—her feet tangled, she twisted her ankle, and then she was hurtling against the table, the edge winding her as it drove into her belly. The axe caught him in the chest, knocking him backwards as the handle shot out of her grasp. Blood splashed her face.

For a moment she lay gasping atop the table, her hand burning. Every wet drop on her skin scalding hot. When she eased herself upright, jagged pain radiated from her shoulders and she tasted bile.

A hand seized her ankle and yanked it forward; her hip cracked against the table as she fell again. She kicked wildly until the hand released her and then scuttled out of reach, pressing her back against the wall as, wheezing, she tried to slow her racing heart.

The Monster was curled on his side, trying fruitlessly to grasp the blood-slicked handle. His hands and chest were drenched, half his face painted red. More blood pooled around him, soaking into her worn rag carpet.

A new thing learned: what it meant to kill a man at close quarters, and in daylight. Watching his mounting terror, smelling his failing body. That her children had each done this, had experienced this moment at such a young age … oh, her grief swelled as it had not done for months, tightening her throat and stinging her eyes. She clenched them shut, pummeling her sorrow back into the depths of her belly, and when she opened her eyes again the Monster was staring at her.

"Not …" he wheezed, more breath than sound. "Not him …"

"Some of us had no choice!" she cried, her voice loud and harsh. "Some of us could only be what you made us!" She crawled forward. "We learned to *do*, General. We learned to kill with our hands and eat corpse-meat like vultures! We did terrible things, my children did terrible things, you made us all Monsters …"

But she was shouting at a corpse.

She dragged him into the fields step by ponderous step, struggling to hold armpits sticky with blood. By the time she dropped him into a weedy patch she was shaking with exhaustion. Every step was a cacophony of pain. She could barely see her house for the gloom of twilight as she stumbled back, leaving both corpse and axe in the wilted grass. In the morning. Everything could wait until the morning.

Inside were the meaty odors of soup and blood. Flies hovered over the stained floorboards. His splattered rucksack had been kicked in a corner. The rug would have to be burned, the floor bleached and scrubbed. It was all she could do to latch the doors and windows and fall into bed.

Alene was wading through the darkened fields, the grass taller than her waist. Everywhere was movement, everywhere she could hear panicked breathing, smell a rank miasma of sweat and blood and urine that blew over her in gusts. The General rose up before her, his face photo-gray, robust in the moonlight and his jacket gleaming with medals. She swung the axe, cutting deep into the scar tissue but she couldn't complete the blow. When she pulled the blade back his head flopped to one side, revealing black, muddy soil beneath. Slowly he crumbled before her, and the axe in her hands was not wood and metal but a clay that cracked in her fist. *Everything's poisoned*, her husband rasped in her ear, the deathbed voice that she had learned not to cringe at. *Even us, we're sick inside now. Nothing good will ever grow here again, Alene. Best to raze it all.* She spooned up soup to silence him; she wasn't ready to listen to him, she would never be ready. Only the soup was heavy, sludgy, and she realized she was feeding him mud and it smelled delicious …

She awoke, cotton-mouthed and disoriented, inhaling over and over the smells of dirt and broth and blood, ears ringing with an incoherent cry. Her arm reached for the side of the bed and she mewled aloud at its emptiness. Only then did she see the stains on her hands and arms. She sat up, sheets pooling around her waist, and saw that she had gone to bed without washing. Past the window, cawing birds circled over the dried grasses; and a crushed trail led back to her house as clearly as a line on a map. Still she felt the dream clinging to her. What were the odds that he would come here, to *this* house? Had she not once also believed, truly believed, that she had seen her daughter walk up the road and into the house, had run back from the field with racing heart and tears in her eyes only to find it empty?

Slowly, stiffly, Alene got out of bed, shaking and pinching herself. The chill in the air setting her skin alight. Outside the birds rose and dropped, jostling for access as they had after the battle, clouds of birds swarming down upon the corpses. But they had drifted away as the land withered and died. Where had these come from, these birds? How far had the smell of dead flesh carried? How starved were they, to cross acres of decay? She felt a strange pang, a mixture of grief and sympathy for these scrawny creatures with their jagged wings, creatures she had once despised.

Not him ...

But it could only have been the Monster. The likeness, his weak denials—impossible that he could be anything but. Her renewed certainty made her first steps out of her bedroom bearable, kept her steady when she saw the great stain on the floor, the spray dotting the walls.

She dragged the blood-stiff rucksack onto the table and began pulling out its contents, all the things she had barely noticed when searching it for weapons. A change of clothes, an empty flask. Dried meat wrapped in a kerchief. A book of prayer, a fancier version of the one she had thrown away, with many phrases underlined:

> *May I never take the blessing of freedom for granted*
> *I am enclosed by wickedness*
> *Give me victory over the corrupt*
> *It is better to trust in the gods than mortal leaders*

She fanned the pages, searching for—what? Some phrase that would confirm it all, that would ease that small nagging doubt—when a photograph fell out.

Three figures in all: an older woman, flanked by two young men. All clearly related, and the men bore the mark of him. A family. Even Monsters, it seemed, had people who loved them, people who would perhaps do to her what she had done to him.

Did they miss him, were they waiting for him? Did they see him walking up to the door, full of life, only to find he was never there?

Alene waited to feel sympathy for this woman like herself, who had perhaps lost children as well as her husband now. But while she could feel something for the birds eating his corpse, she could feel nothing for the woman who had shared his bed.

And what did it matter? He was dead; it was done. Just another corpse among thousands.

As she put aside the rucksack, however, she heard the sound of a motor in the distance. Not the stuttering engines of one of the dilapidated vehicles from town; this was a steady, well-maintained purr.

Alene looked at the stained floor and walls, her

own filthy body. So lost in her reverie and now there was no time. A swift, fleeting panic ran through her: she must concoct a plausible story, perhaps a third party who had followed him and attacked him in the night …

But as swiftly as it began, the panic faded, and she merely went to the sink. She washed her hands and face and combed her hair; she checked the buttons on her dress, that there were no unsightly gaps. A turning point, when you no longer cared enough to dissemble. A point from which there was no coming back.

Nothing good will ever grow here again, Alene.

The vehicle turned out to be an official-looking little truck. It stopped at her door; the two soldiers that came out had ribbons on their jackets and carried sidearms, but they flushed like schoolboys when she opened the door. So young! As young as her own had been when they first left, before they understood what they were giving themselves over to.

"Very sorry to intrude," one said, holding up a photo. "We're looking for this man."

The gaunt man from her table stared at her, clad only in a thin, sleeveless shirt. The scarring, she saw now, extended over his shoulder and down his chest, like it had been splashed onto him. In black and white the resemblance was even stronger, but now the tiniest differences leapt out at her. The thinness of his lips— hadn't the General's mouth been fuller, kinder? Was the anger in the staring eyes from being captured, or from being mistaken for another?

Was the scarring a poor attempt to mar the original cut, or a terrible coincidence?

"This man is wanted for questioning regarding his wartime activities," the other soldier continued, clearly reciting. "All participants will be held accountable. Every citizen is expected to help or suffer the consequences of collaboration."

The taste of the broth came back to her, the familiarity of it. Were they speaking of the General? Had they been ordered to vagueness? Her feet were still grimy with blood and dirt. Or perhaps they did not know who they hunted?

We're sick inside now. Nothing good will ever grow here again, Alene.

"He's in the back," she said.

They blinked in astonishment, hands dropping to their holsters. One gestured for her to come out, but she only smiled wearily at him. "He's in the field," she corrected. "He'll give you no trouble."

The soldiers exchanged a look; then they ran around the house, pistols drawn. She watched them run, the early morning light glinting off their helmets, and for a moment they were her son and his friends, wrestling and mock-fighting in the thick, waving wheat …

Best to raze it all.

She took a bowl of water and cloth into the bedroom and washed thoroughly, then put on her most handsome dress. Everything was poisoned, and perhaps it had been for longer than she had realized. How quickly had her daughter enlisted, with her husband's encouragement? How had Alene struggled to keep her son home for one last precious year, despite his anguish at being kept from the fighting? All of them so eager to kill, even her husband in his old age, even herself.

She had never unpacked the suitcase she had prepared after her son's letter came. Now she dusted it and placed it by the door. In the field she could hear the soldiers arguing, probably about what to do.

It could only be him. But to send two boys, to find the most fearsome of their leaders?

It could only be him.

When at last one came back inside he took off his helmet, but also kept his pistol half-raised, as if he wasn't sure whether to beg her pardon or shoot her. "Who else was here yesterday?" he asked, a hint of pleading in his voice.

"No one," she said, then, before he could reply: "It is *him*, isn't it? The Monster?"

He just looked at her blankly. The woman in the photograph, the grown sons. *You could not tell her from a butcher's scraps.* "It's just that everything is poisoned now," she said. "You, me, the very earth we stand on. And the things we've done—!" At his growing unease she leaned over and patted his arm. "Not you, of course," she amended.

The soldier glanced over his shoulder, at his fellow who had appeared in the doorway; the latter made a little *go on* gesture.

"Ma'am," he said carefully, turning back to her, "I'm very sorry to say I must arrest you—"

"Of course you must." She patted his arm again. "Only—could you bring me back here, after? To the fields. The birds will be so hungry ..." She picked up the case and slipped her shoes on, then looked from one to the other. "It was him, wasn't it? Of course you cannot say. But it was him, I'm certain of it. I learned to do, after all. A Monster just like he was."

TO US MAY GRACE BE GIVEN

1.

THEY CAME near the end of the day. We thought it was thunder at first, though there weren't any clouds. Eight of them on horseback with Bill Boyland at their head. "Eight men for a woman and her kid," Mam muttered as she loaded the revolver.

Once they came through our gate, they stayed in their saddles. I couldn't see their faces for their hats pulled low; I only recognized Bill Boyland by his voice and the shiny gold watch hanging from his waistcoat. He told us Mam's letter and papers didn't matter none. Mam started arguing with him. I couldn't speak because my voice would give me away as a girl.

"Your Pa was a squatter," Bill Boyland said to me. He spoke slow, like I was thickheaded. "Now your Ma is right: ten years ago it didn't matter none, because ten years ago it was every man for himself. But that was then."

"And this is now, and you're nothing but a god-damned thief, William Boyland," Mam said.

"Constance, I warned you and Matthew both. This land *deceives*. It looks good but the dirt's cruel. Doesn't matter how much you pray over it, it's never gonna be good for anything but making meat." His hat nodded at me. "You're working your boy like a god-damned animal, and for what? You both deserve better than this."

"Better than our God-given home?" Mam asked. "Better than what's rightfully ours? I have blood in this land, William Boyland, blood and ten years' honest work—not that you would know anything about that."

A few of the men muttered when she spoke, but Bill Boyland raised his hand and they silenced quick. "Only the Land Office can give the homes out here, Constance. You should have filed claim—as you say, you had ten years to do it in." He hadn't raised his voice once. "Now I bought this land fair and square, Missus Norton, and I mean to have it. I want you gone before the next full moon."

When they had ridden away, I let the knife slide out from my sleeve and Mam untucked the revolver from beneath her apron. She went in the house, leaving me to put away the loys. I made out like I was tired from plowing, but in truth I worked slow because I thought my heart might burst from beating so hard. Eight men. We had the revolver and the shotgun, but we were close to being out of cartridges for both. Mam hadn't wanted to go to town for weeks now. She was afraid Bill would have a man watching, who would come after she was gone and rob us blind and do worse to me. But I knew now that was a mistake. Eight men and he could probably come back with double as quick as you please, and it was less than a month to the full moon.

When I finally went in, she had cleared the table and pulled the carpetbag out from under the bed. It was grey with dust. Even before Da died Mam and I weren't supposed to touch it, though I used to open it when no one was looking. *It's the past*, Da would say when I asked him about it. *From when we thought we knew better than God. We came here to get away from that.*

The way Mam was laying things out, I knew I wasn't the only one who had peeked inside. She didn't even have to look, just put out the candles and the fancy drawings, and even the vials that I liked best. In your hand the stuff inside looked black, but when you held them up to the light you saw that it was really a dark, sweet red.

Beside these, Mam put a knife I had never seen before, with a thick handle and two round blades folded up like a flower.

"I'll show him," she said. "I'll show him my god-damned claim."

"What d'you mean?" I asked. My voice sounded funny. Sometimes I went so long without speaking I forgot what I sounded like.

Mam didn't answer. She was peering at the drawings, holding them up to the light and talking to herself.

I started cutting up the potatoes for supper, but I kept looking at that knife. Not round, the blades; more like petals, tight as a spring bud. I reached out and touched the handle only to jump when the blades snapped apart. Now it looked like jaws ready to bite.

"Leave it be," Mam said. She bundled everything up again and went back out into the yard. Under the beech tree she began dragging her heel in the dirt, making a circle.

I followed her outside. "Mam, what're you doing?"

She grinned at me then, not her nice smile, but the way she smiled when we killed rats in the barn.

"Calling down the god-damned devil on that sonofabitch Boyland," she said, and got down on her hands and knees in the circle.

We had nearly three weeks before Bill Boyland was to come back, but as Mam explained it, sometimes the devil takes a while. We took turns watching the circle and keeping up with the plowing. Mam said it wasn't a circle but a kind of snare. She had put the last of our salt pork in the middle and kept adding drops from one of the vials to it, her face getting grimmer by the day. I didn't know why we didn't just send the devil to Bill Boyland direct, rather than bring him to us. What if the devil decided to take us all? But Mam didn't look like she was for questioning, so instead I said that the goats might get at the bait.

"Nah, Addy. It's devil's blood." She touched my shoulder, which made me feel better. "The goats are smart, they know better than to touch it."

"The devil will come for his own blood." My voice nearly twisted up, making it a question, but I caught myself in time. Mam was fierce with the whip when she got the rage in her.

"They'll come to rescue one of their kind," she said. "They won't come for food, they can get that anywhere. But they'll come for one of their own. Any of them within a hundred miles, they'll smell it."

And then I really wanted to ask questions, because I had always thought there was just one devil, the one in the Bible. Now I pictured devils like rabbits, with horns for ears and long sharp tails. I wanted to ask Mam how many devils there were, and did they come in different kinds, and what if we got the wrong one? But she was smiling the rat-killing grin again, and all those questions weren't really what I wanted to ask: If a devil came, what was to stop him killing us as well?

That night I took a while feeding the goats. They crowded around all warm and nibbled my fingers. We had to sell most of the animals when Da died, but Mam had made sure we kept the goats and the chickens. I watched the goats being born every year, and the ones I had to nurse I named in my head, though I never told Mam. When they grew too old for milking or making babies she would walk them down the road a ways to a fellow named Tom. He had a big herd that he rented out for clearing brush, sometimes even for the railroad. In the post office there was a print of the railroad coming through, and I would pretend our goats were just past the edge of the paper, eating up the dead grass and keeping the men safe from fire.

I whispered their names now as I fed them. Isaac, after one of my favorite stories. Leah and Rachel, because their story always made me feel sad, and I thought they would have been happier without Jacob. There had been one I named Matthew, after my Da, but he was with Tom now. Cain and Abel, for twins that kept butting each other. Even a little Addy, because she came so late like I had done.

If Bill Boyland got the land, we'd have to sell them all, maybe to someone for their meat.

Isaac butted my hand and I scratched his head. I knew him by his uneven horns. I knew them all and they all knew me, they would come when I called them. Mam wanted to keep the land because it was ours, because Da had cleared it and worked it until it killed him. But I wanted to keep the land for Mam and the goats, so we could all stay together.

I looked at Mam, sitting on the edge of the circle, waiting for the devil to come. Anything, to keep us here, together. Anything.

It was six days and nights before the devil finally came.

2.

The devil came up over the hill at sunset, hunched over and leading a lame horse. It wore a hat and coat like anyone. I thought it was one of Bill Boyland's men, but Mam hissed *at last* and went behind the house. I didn't know what to do, so I just stood there on the far side of the beech and waited.

It approached slow, like it sensed something was wrong. I couldn't see its face for the kerchief over its mouth. At the fence it stopped and waved at me. I waved back before I thought better of it, but there was nothing for it then.

Halfway across the yard, it stopped again and looked around. I could see its eyes squinting, could see its nose wrinkle as it smelled the bait. It turned completely, looking back at the fence, and that was when Mam ran out of nowhere with the jaw-blades and drove them into the devil's back, right between the shoulders, and snapped them shut.

It screamed then, its voice as high as my own, and fell like it'd been shot. The horse reared and ran to the far side of the yard.

"Get the little yoke," Mam said.

The devil's hat had fallen off. Its long brown hair fell everywhere, thick and snaking. There was a big stain on its back where the handle stuck out, and blood was dripping on the ground. With a moan it started to drag itself back towards the fence, hand over hand, its legs twisting up.

"Addy, get the god-damn yoke!" Mam yelled.

I ran to the barn. The devil was cursing now, calling Mam terrible names, and I clapped my hands over my ears. It took me a while to find the little yoke, the one Da had made for our last, runty ox. When I came back out Mam had her knee on the devil's backside and was holding its head down with one hand, pushing aside its hair with the other.

Her head, *her* hair. I didn't know much about devils, but now that I was close, I could see this one looked an awful lot like a woman.

"Look," Mam said. She dug her nails into the devil's neck, making her shriek into the dirt, and scraped something free. When she held out her hand to me there were shiny circles on her fingers. "Child of the serpent. You would never know it to look at her. For generations your Da's people fought 'em, to the death more often than not. Now she can start paying us back."

My mouth was hanging open and I closed it tight.

The devil said something then. Mam lifted her hand away and the devil twisted her head to look at me. She looked like a woman, but her face was all hollow and a sickly gray, like she was ill. Her eyes were the same dark brown as mine.

"You've made a terrible mistake," she said.

"That may be," Mam said, "but it's done now." She took the yoke from me and latched it round the devil's neck.

We tied the devil up in a stall in the barn, tying the yoke to the walls and her wrists to the yoke and hobbling her feet just to be sure. When I reached for the blade, Mam slapped my hand and shook her head. The devil's legs were still limp. She hadn't fought when we dragged her across the yard, just looked from me to Mam and back again. Even knowing about the snakeskin, she still didn't look like a devil to me. She looked like a woman, sick and scared.

"Please," she said now. "Please, I can't feel anything. Just get me a doctor and I won't tell anyone, I promise." Her eyes looked wet. "I have family waiting for me, they'll pay whatever you want."

Mam just snorted and checked the knots.

"My name is Elisabeth," she said, turning to me. She was crying; my own throat got tight. "Please, I have no money, why are you doing this? Please send for a doctor. I can't feel my legs, oh God, why are you doing this?"

"Mam," I whispered.

"You can save your breath." Mam said. "We'll let you go after the next full moon." She jerked her head at the doors. "Men are going to come here, they've threatened me and my boy. You take care of them for us and we'll let you go."

The devil just looked at her, her eyes huge and weeping.

"If you don't, I'll take your blood and do the job myself."

Still the devil just looked at her. I could see her trembling.

"Well," Mam said. "We best get supper on."

"Wait!" She leaned forward. "You can't just leave me here! I may never walk again!"

Mam laughed. "If I took that blade out you'd have my throat before I could take a breath."

"Mam," I whispered again. She looked like she was hurting bad. What if we had made a mistake, what if we were killing her?

But Mam patted my arm. "It's all right, Addy. Think about it. If she were what she claims to be she'd have bled out by now. She sure as hell wouldn't have the strength to holler like that." She turned towards the barn doors. "Come on. We've done a good day's work."

"No, you mustn't leave me! Please!" The devil was looking at me, all wild and sobbing. "I just want a doctor. For God's sake! I'll do whatever you want, just send for a doctor!"

I bit my lip. I felt like I might cry too, but Mam hated tears. Only how could a devil even say *God* without getting struck down? "What if we're wrong?" I whispered. "What if she's just a person?"

Mam sighed then and crouched down in front of the stall, plucking at the old straw. "I know what you are," she said to the devil. "Matthew's da was an alchemist and a preacher, as was his da, all the way back to Thomas Norton himself. Matthew told me the real story of Eden, how the serpent tricked Eve so he could eat from the tree of life, and how all his offspring carry that in their blood. Mankind's birthright gobbled right up. But it wasn't all good, was it?" She smiled at the devil. "No, it came with all sorts of problems. Like your hunger, like how a little knife can leave you helpless. Like how even a foolish old woman can make a poison that will turn you to dust."

At Mam's words the devil's eyes went hard, and her mouth became a line. She met Mam's gaze square, and then she spat in the straw.

"That's what I think of your fucking das," she said. "Cruel madmen to a one. Rather like you, I suspect." All the trembling and fear were gone. "So your *plan*—" She made the word sound dirty. "—is to keep me tied up until the next full moon, and then what? I can't *walk*, you idiot."

"Not now you can't," Mam said. "But we both know it's only the blade—"

"No, *you* know that," the devil interrupted, and Mam's face went dark. "I will tell you what *I* know, shall I? I know that if I don't feed soon, I'll be dead by the time your men come. I know that if you don't give me time to heal after you remove the blade I will be nothing more than another bitch for them to fuck and kill. And I know you are in no way strong enough to drink *my* blood, not with that sickness in you."

I stepped back, expecting Mam to go in a rage, but she didn't. She didn't even speak. She only stayed crouched, with her face dark and her hands twisting in her skirts, and then I was proper afraid. No one had ever spoken to her like that without her raging at them.

"Now your daughter here, she might be able to drink," the devil continued, looking at me. The line of her mouth curled up and it was awful. "You're as strong as a little horse, aren't you? A god-damned mule of a girl. So your mother's the mouth and you're the muscle, is that how it is?"

"That's my son," Mam said then, but her voice was something I'd never heard before, all strained and cracked.

"I have given you the courtesy of my honesty," the devil said. "I recommend you do the same." She leaned forward again. "I've met your kind before, missus. You listen in on your menfolk, you sneak into their studies and read their books, and you think you know better than they did, and you always die worse." She kept talking when Mam started to speak. "If you took the blade out now it would be days before I could walk again, and my belly was empty long before now. Even if you hadn't crippled me, I'd barely be able to stand. I need at least three nights to heal and I need to eat. So put *that* in your fucking plan."

Mam bared her teeth, then reached over and smacked my leg. "Go start supper," she said. "Go on, now. I got business here to take care of."

Just before the barn doors I looked back. Mam was saying something to the devil, something I couldn't make out. What if it was true, what the devil said? What if Mam had read the book wrong, what if there was some kind of sickness in her? She was always tired, but we were both always tired, there was only the two of us to do everything.

Mam kept talking, her face was whipping mean. If the devil replied at all I couldn't hear it, and I didn't want to.

From the kitchen window, I watched as Mam stormed out of the barn, cursing and kicking at the dirt, the shotgun in her hand. I thought to hide then but she went to the horse instead, seizing its reins and dragging it limping past the fence where she shot it in the head. I could have sworn I heard a cry from the barn, but it could have been me. Just to shoot it like that, when it might have only needed shoeing. Just to shoot it. Mam stripped off the saddle and harness and as she was passing the barn she threw them in a heap by the door and then I did hear something, not a cry but the devil cursing like when Mam first stabbed her. She kept on long after Mam started the evening chores and I was making supper; she kept on until at last she just stopped, like someone had cut her throat.

"I don't think she can stop all Bill Boyland's men," I said to Mam when she came in for supper.

"She will if she wants to live," Mam said. "You just stay away from her. She's got a mouth on her, that one."

I stirred the soup, trying to think how to ask without asking.

"I get pains in my stomach, Addy," Mam said then. "They come and go. Sometimes I sick up and there's blood. That's why it has to be this way. This land is all you'll have after I'm gone. A woman can't get by without money or a man. This land is as good as dollars."

I heard her, but at the same time it seemed like she was speaking from a long way away. Tears kept coming out and I watched as they fell into the pot, making little circles in the soup. I didn't dare sniffle or let on how I felt. It would only get me slapped.

"Maybe we should explain more," I finally said when I could talk again. "Maybe we could pay her with some land. Maybe then she would want to help us."

"Addy, she's a devil." Mam sighed. "The moment we take that knife out she'll kill whatever's to hand. We just gotta make sure that's Bill Boyland and not us."

3.

The next day I started the planting. It felt strange to be working, but as Mam said, it would be something to find ourselves rid of Bill Boyland only to starve next winter. I carefully tossed the seed onto the ground, whispering the prayers Da had taught me. Mam had mixed the seed sack the night before, adding the special powder Da had brought with us. He had said that the powder and praying made the ground more willing. We were nearly out of the powder now, but I wasn't sure it mattered. Each year the crops were mean, enough to keep us alive but not enough to sell.

I thought Mam was going to follow me with the harrow, but instead she went into the goat pen with a rope. I stopped and watched her. The goats had been upset that morning; the horse was starting to smell and it was scaring them. Had they done something? I tried to see Mam but she was bent over. There was a lot of bleating and then she stood up again, leading one of the goats out and kicking the pen shut. I could just make out his uneven horns. She didn't lead Isaac to the road, towards Tom's place; instead she led him over to the water pump and the half-log where Da had done his cleaning. I didn't understand; why did she need to give him water? I had filled all the troughs fresh this morning.

I didn't understand, but then I saw the knife and the bowl, and then Mam seized Isaac by the larger horn. An awful sound filled the air, a kind of bleating but worse, as if he was screaming. I opened my mouth but there was only the screaming. I was running and halfway to the log Mam dragged the knife across his neck and his skin peeled open and the screaming became blood.

When I reached the log the thing on it was Isaac and not. He was some other kind of animal, something that had a throat gaping loose and bloody and a tongue hanging out. *Isaac*, I said, but nothing came out, like she had cut my throat too.

Mam steadied the bowl under him, catching every

drop of his bright, bright blood. It was so cold. Behind us the other goats bucked against the wall of their pen and bleated and I tried to say *Isaac* again but I was shivering too much. It was so very cold.

"Idiot," Mam yelled, "you're dropping seed everywhere!"

I looked down and in my hand was the sack of seed and what was left was spilling onto the ground. I got down and picked up the seeds one by one until they were just a blur. Mam hated tears. I scraped at the dirt, feeling for the little shapes. Isaac. Everything went dark and I looked up to see Mam standing over me, the bowl on her hip stinking of blood.

"I don't dare take it to Tom," she said. "Skin it and quarter it; we'll figure out what to do with the meat later."

I couldn't speak for the pain in my throat, like there was a fist pressing everything down into my belly.

"What's wrong?" She frowned at me and I shrank back, swallowing and swallowing.

"Tom?" I finally croaked.

"Of course, Tom." Her frown deepened. "Why, who else would we sell the carcass to?"

"I—I thought," I said, but I couldn't say any more. I hadn't thought. I had never thought.

"Are you thinking of that herd he sold to the railroads? There hasn't been anything like that for years now. More's the pity, he charged them a fortune for the lot, said they were getting the brush cleared and a winter's worth of meat besides." She laughed.

"Shrewd old bastard. That was a good Christmas, do you remember? You ate yourself sick on the candy your Da bought." Steadying the bowl, she leaned over and touched my cheek. "Now be a help and skin it. I'll clean it and make a nice stew. We still have plenty of onions."

She went into the barn, bracing the bowl as she worked the door open and closed. As soon as the door shut I pressed my hand over my mouth so she wouldn't hear the noises pushing up. From the pen, the goats bleated softly, as if they heard me, as if they understood.

When I stood up the smell of the horse blew over me, now mixed with the smell of Isaac. The first vultures were circling. I hated the devil then, I hated her for coming and I hated Mam for calling her, I hated the land and the house and even the goats for making me like them. I took up the knife. Isaac looked small on the half-log, not much bigger than the bowl Mam had bled him into. I touched him and he was warm and his hair felt just like it had that morning. I remembered when he was born, how I had dried him and nursed him. I started crying hard, because I hated him too, but I also loved him, and I wished I was the one on the wood instead of him.

The barn window was open. Mam suddenly said in her cold voice, the voice before she got angry, "You'll drink it and you'll like it."

The devil started laughing. "I can't drink that," she said. "It's worse than water."

"It's all I got."

"Then you should have fucking thought of that beforehand!" the devil screamed. Her voice was so loud the chickens took up squawking.

There was a thump and the crack of the whip, over and over. I flinched and started to reach for Isaac, but there wasn't any reason to protect him now.

"I don't need you!" Mam roared, the worst I'd heard in ages. "I only need what's in your veins, damn you!"

"Then come and take it," the devil yelled, and there was no fear in her voice.

The barn door flew open and Mam came out. Blood was splashed all down her front; the empty bowl hung from her hands. Without looking at me she stomped back to the house, throwing the bowl against the side before she went in. It left a red stain on the wall.

I looked down at Isaac's little body. Killed for nothing. Killed for nothing. What harm had he ever done anyone?

I pressed hard on my mouth, but the sound of crying didn't stop. Only then did I realize that it was coming from the barn, that the devil was crying too.

It took me all afternoon to skin Isaac. I'd never done such a bad job of anything. I kept saying *I'm sorry I'm sorry* until I wasn't sure if it was for letting Mam kill him, or for making such a mess of him after he was gone.

At supper I couldn't eat. The stew was the color of dried blood and had pieces of meat and onion floating in it and just looking at it made my stomach hurt. Even worse was looking up at the cutting block, where I could still see his little feet. I tried to spoon up just the broth but pieces of meat kept coming in. The stew tasted like sick and sorrow; even in tiny amounts it all kept coming back up.

We sat in silence until suddenly Mam spoke. "Adelaide Norton, I'm only going to say this once." She spoke quiet, like someone was sleeping nearby. "You have got to stop this. You're not a child anymore. If you're this soft over an animal, what will you do when Bill Boyland's men start blubbering for their lives? You show them an ounce of mercy and they will cut you dead. That is the world, Adelaide. There is nothing out there——" She pointed her spoon at the window. "——that will spare you at their own expense, not Bill Boyland and not that thing in the barn and not even your god-damned goats. This world isn't founded on mercy. It is founded on survival, and God helps those who help themselves. Now you eat that god-damn stew or so help me I'll make you."

Slowly I spooned up a piece of meat, watching it shudder in its little puddle of broth, and put it in my mouth. Sick and sorrow. I swallowed it whole, and when my stomach twisted I imagined the fist inside me pressing it down so it couldn't come back up.

"Better," Mam said. "Someday you'll see that I'm

doing this for you. Someday you'll see just how close we came to dying out here."

That night I couldn't sleep for thinking. My hands felt sticky with blood though I had washed them clean. There were flies in the house and Mam was snoring and finally I got out of bed and went out into the yard.

Everything was quiet and still. There were so many stars above the black hills, their light made the grass look like silver. The air tasted like the smell of the horse, rotting where it had fallen. Something was chewing on it, a lean shadow that smacked its lips as it ate. I felt small. I went to the goat pen and watched them sleeping, and I thought of Isaac and hoped he was happy up in the stars, running and playing and eating whatever he wanted. I thought of his dark eyes and his little horns and how he knew me, how he would always come to me instead of Mam. He knew me.

In the barn, it was silent, but in a different way. The way it's silent when you hold your breath.

"Are you all right?" I asked, for something to say.

She seemed to be asleep but then I saw her eyes were open. She didn't say anything, so I crouched down like Mam had done and picked at the straw. The ropes creaked and when I looked at the devil, she was looking at me. Her face was even thinner and bruised now too, and there were stains on her torn shirt and coat.

"I've had better days." Her voice was rough. "Is it your turn, then? Like mother, like daughter? Or perhaps you're like your father, you want to cut me up and see what makes me tick?"

"Da never hurt anyone," I said. "He came out here so he wouldn't have to hurt people anymore. He said people were supposed to make the world balanced. Like morning and night, or wild and tame things. That way God would give us His grace again."

"Does this look like fucking balance to you?" She looked at me so hard I flinched. "Why were you crying before?"

I knew I shouldn't tell her anything, but I felt desperate to speak. "The goat, the one Mam ..." I couldn't say *killed*. "His name was Isaac," I finally got out.

"I'm sorry, Addy." And she did sound sorry, truly sorry.

I sat down completely then. "If you promised to help us," I said, "I could try to get Mam to take the knife out."

"I think your mother and I are past the point of bargains." She lunged forward, so suddenly I yelped. "But *we* could bargain."

Her fingertips curled towards my face and I jerked back, crawling until I hit one of the barn posts. Her eyes weren't brown anymore; they were black and flat and huge. "Your mother needs me alive, Addy. That means she'll keep killing your livestock, because she is desperate and there is nothing else she will give me." Her lip curled up in the corner. "But you could give me something."

I opened my mouth, but all that came out was, "What?"

"You're starting to bleed." She said the word with a sigh, like it was a fellow she was sweet on. "Bring me your blood, and I'll tell her I can drink something else —rats, or maybe chickens. Your goats, at least, will be safe."

I gaped at her. "Why would you want *that*?"

She leaned back, smiling. Her teeth were bright with moonlight and it was terrible.

"It's … it's disgusting." Just the thought made me shudder. I couldn't even look at the rags, Mam always washed them for me.

At that her smile broadened. "But it's part of being a woo-man."

"Doesn't make it nice," I said. "Besides, nothing else does that. Only people."

"Sadly, we must live in the bodies we are given."

"But you dress like a boy," I pointed out.

At that the devil laughed, soft and bitter. "You meet all kinds out here." Before I could say something she added, "But I don't think you dress this way out of fear, do you? You *like* boy's clothes."

"Don't you?" I'd seen the women in town, stuck on porches to stay out of the sun, talking about dresses and husbands. They couldn't even ride horses. "I wouldn't even know how to wear a dress now. I haven't been a girl since I was little."

"Did your mother decide that?"

"She cut my hair and took away my dresses when we came out here. Told Da to call me his son. He didn't like it, though. He always said—" I took a breath. It felt funny to be talking about something so long ago. "He always said by the time I grew up there would be more folks out here, good folks, and I could go back to being a girl again."

"Well," the devil said, "I can see your mother once had some sense." Her smile became sly. "Though it would be a pity to put you back in a dress. You wear those pants quite well."

Her words made me go hot all over. For a moment I felt all sorts of strange things, things I didn't want to think about. What had Mam said? *She has a mouth on her.* I got to my feet; I needed air.

"Strong as a mule and a rare kind of lovely," the devil said, watching me. "Now we'll see if *you* have any sense, eh? Bring me your blood, Addy. Bring me your rags. Because without them, you, your Mam, your goats ..." She dragged her finger across her throat.

"I can't," I said. "Mam might find out, she'd whip us both."

"Oh, you're a clever girl—" I started walking away as she talked. She broke off and called "Addy!"

Like a fool, I looked back. She was leaning forward again, just visible past the edge of the stall. She wasn't smiling anymore.

"What did your mother do with your Isaac, hmm?"

Out of nowhere, the fist filled my throat, so fast my eyes stung, pressing so hard I thought I would burst.

"Is your belly full of your little friend? Your friend who trusted you, who thought of you like you were *his* Mam, until *your* Mam cut his throat?"

And I could hear Isaac screaming again. I could see his head as the skin had come away and how, when I brought him in the house, Mam had slapped his body on the table and brought the cleaver up and down, up and down—

I ran out of the barn sobbing. I ran until I was at the beech tree and there I sat, crying and crying, thinking of nursing him in my lap, how quickly he had grown. *Isaac, Isaac!* I mouthed his name until it was nonsense and then I wept more.

It was dawn before I finally went back to bed. I felt nothing inside, nothing. I was as dead as he was.

4.

The next day I woke up aching with my monthlies, just as the devil had said. Mam bled out a chicken and went to the barn. I felt sick inside, thinking of what the devil might say to Mam, but there were no fights or hollering. When Mam came back out the bowl was empty, but she wasn't smiling. "Sicked up most of it," she said when I followed her into the kitchen. She was plucking the chicken so hard she ripped a wing half off. "We'll have to try again tomorrow."

I nodded. I had decided to say as little as I could,

in case I gave away about going to the barn, but I knew that Mam was totting up the days and the animals just as I was. *Put that in your fucking plan.* I was, and it wasn't adding up.

That night I watched the moon rise. Just a thin curve of white in the sky, nearly all blotted out. But soon it would grow fat and full, and then they would come, and even if we kept the devil alive that long, what if she chose to help Bill Boyland instead of us? For the first time in a long time, I wished, really wished, that Da was still alive, so he could tell Mam if she was doing right or not.

After supper, Mam sat down at the table with the carpetbag again. She read one of the papers carefully, then opened up some of the other vials and mashed their contents in the mortar until they made a black paste. When she saw me watching she said, "Poison."

"For who?" I asked.

"For the devil, who d'you think?" She laughed, low and bitter. "If I could get away with poisoning Bill Boyland, I'd have done it years ago. Would've saved this whole territory a lot of grief."

I sat down across from her. "How will you get her to take it?"

"I won't. We shoot it into her." She heated the tip of an awl and made a little hollow in one of the bullets. With a spoon she pushed in the paste and scraped it smooth, then put it on the table. "Let it dry. It only takes a little. Turns their blood to powder." She squinted again at the paper as she picked up a second cartridge. "No, sand, I think it says sand.

That'll be something, eh? Cut her and watch her pour out like a sack of flour."

"What if it doesn't work?" I asked.

At that her face grew dark. "I got her here, didn't I? I've got a god-damned devil tied up in our barn, how many times have you seen that before? When your great-grandda would hunt them he would take six men with him, and still they would get killed often as not." She shook her head. "You need to ask less and do more. Now go to bed."

I got under the covers, listening to Mam singing under her breath:

> *The Son of God goes forth to war,*
> *a kingly crown to gain;*
> *his blood red banner streams afar:*
> *who follows in his train?*
> *Who best can drink his cup of woe,*
> *triumphant over pain,*
> *who patient bears his cross below,*
> *he follows in his train.*

I gave myself over to thinking, about what little we had and what might happen when Bill Boyland came. Mam seemed to be fixing to break her word to the devil, and that didn't seem like it could lead to anything good. And even if she killed the devil, even if we got rid of her and Bill Boyland and all his men, we still wouldn't have a proper deed to the land.

When Mam finally came to bed I listened carefully to her breathing, and then I went out to the

barn with my stained rags wadded in my hand.
There wasn't much blood yet, but I didn't want to
wait. It felt important not to wait. In the distance I
could hear things crawling in the horse's bones,
could hear the goats nervous in their pen, but I
didn't dare try to comfort them in case the noise
woke up Mam.

It wasn't silent in the barn this time. There was a
wheezing sound, long and low. In the stall the devil
was slumped in the yoke. She looked all bone in the
moonlight; she looked like she was dead, until I heard
again the slow wheeze of her breath.

I held out the rags and her head lifted. Her eyes
were slits. She opened her hand but didn't move so I
had to step close to give it to her. The moment her
fingers closed around them I hurried back to the edge
of the stall.

She sniffed them, and then pressed the stains to
her lips and began sucking on them. It made me feel
queer, frightened and kind of excited all at once. I
wanted to run, but I made myself stay put. After all,
we had a bargain.

After a while she stopped sucking and licked the
cloths instead, turning them one way and another and
wetting every spot.

"Ahhh." She licked a last spot and looked at me.
Her face was less gray, though she still looked sickly.
"Thank you, Addy."

I nearly said *you're welcome*. But she was a devil
after all. "Will you help us when Bill Boyland comes?"
I asked instead.

She leaned back in the yoke, closing her eyes. "Tell me about your Boyland."

"He's a big cattle rancher. He owns most of the land around here. What he doesn't use for his cattle he rents out to farmers. He even owns the land under the inn and the bank. The lawyer says he exhorts everyone."

"Ex-*torts*," the devil said. "Him and half the men in this territory."

"Bill Boyland says Mam didn't file claim, so he bought the land fair and square, but Mam went to the lawyer and he said she has papers showing she was here first. Only she's afraid to go to the city for a judge because she thinks Bill Boyland will just take the land while we're gone. She got a letter from the lawyer instead, but Bill Boyland says that's not good enough."

"Then send the lawyer for the judge," the devil said.

I frowned. "I don't think we can."

"You didn't go to this lawyer?"

"I had to take care of things here."

The devil pursed her lips at this, but said nothing.

"Maybe the lawyer's frightened Bill Boyland will have him shot," I said. "That's what happened with the last farmer who tried to keep his land. Bill Boyland went out there with his men and they shot them all, and they shot the lawyer so he wouldn't tell anyone what they'd done. Then they burned all the buildings so there would be no papers, so when the judge finally came there was nothing."

"Thorough," the devil said.

"Mam says you can kill them for us."

At that she laughed. "Your Mam talks a lot of shit."

"She called you here," I said.

"She didn't call me here. I was on my way to the city and my horse went lame. I was partial to that horse," she added, and there was a tremor in her voice now. "You're not the only one who lost a friend in this."

I didn't want to think about that. "But she baited the circle—"

"Oh, I smelled your rotten meat. When I was inside your fence, not a hundred miles away." She smiled at me, a nice smile. "The way I hear it, I'm supposed to be descended from a snake, not a goddamned dog."

Before I could catch myself I smiled back at her.

"Look, Addy." The smile went quick. "Your blood will keep me alive but little more. Even if you took out the blade right now? It would be days before I could walk, much less help you fight anyone." She met my eyes square. "If your Boyland is honest, he'll be here at the full moon. But if he's not? He'll be here a hell of a lot sooner, or he'll send men out here instead."

"Why?" I asked, startled.

"Because that way he can kill you both, and then come back at the full moon with plenty of witnesses and oh dear, it must have been thieves, that's what happens when women homestead without a man, what a pity."

She was right. He could do it. I could *see* him doing it. She was right.

"If you truly want me to help you? I need more blood, a lot of it, and I need that damn knife out. Now, preferably."

I hesitated then, trying to think. "Mam says she can drink yours and take care of Bill——"

"If your Mam drank my blood she would keel over dead," the devil said, as reasonably as if we were discussing planting. "And if you drank my blood you might keel over dead, but if not? You would become a devil like me, and to be honest I don't think you're cut out for it."

I hesitated again. Now I wished I hadn't come. Mam was right, she did have a mouth on her, one that said confusing things.

"The blood you need," I said slowly, "it's people's blood, isn't it? Not chickens or goats or anything else."

She just looked at me.

"But there's no one for miles except me and Mam."

"I don't make the rules, Addy," she said. "That's just how it is."

I swallowed. Horrible, confusing things, but I understood that well enough. No one made the rules about land either, or about folks like Bill Boyland trying to do you out of it.

"How long do you think we have?" I asked.

"He said by the full moon?" At my nod she smiled again. "Then I'd say it could be any time now. Right now, it's nice and dark outside, and all sorts of things can happen in the dark. It's long enough before that he could make up a good story about where he was, but not so far ahead that they won't recognize you. Right about now would be a perfect time."

I nodded again, my head jerking up and down like I was one of the chickens. *Right about now.* I thought I could hear hoofbeats.

"I'll try to do something," I said, though I couldn't think what. "I'll try," I said again.

The devil waved the sodden rags at me and I took them quick, swiping them out of her hand. Her skin looked gray again. Silently I backed out of the barn and into the silvery yard. I looked around before cutting across, as if Bill Boyland might already be there, ready to shoot me dead.

Back in bed I thought it through again. There had been another family, far to the east, right where they were setting the county line. Thieves had cut them up and burnt their house and barn both. At the time, everyone had just said what a shame it was, but I wondered now, because Bill Boyland had bought that land at auction right after. He had divided it up and rented the lots to eight different families, where before there had only been one.

Extort. I saw now that Mam and I were nothing compared to that, nothing compared to rectangles of land where people paid just to be allowed to live.

I held my arm up to the moonlight, looking at the lines of blood under my skin. We were nothing to Bill Boyland, but we could be something to the devil, maybe enough of a something to help when the time came. I just had to figure how I could bleed myself without dying.

That night I dreamed I was crouched by the beech tree, keeping watch over the circle, waiting for the devil to come. I picked at the bark and the sap ran, only it wasn't sap but blood; I picked more bark off and underneath was goat hair. I heard bleating then. I pulled and pulled at the bark and underneath were the goats, all of them cut up and bleeding and stuffed inside the tree like sausage meat. They were all dying and when I tried to pull them out my hands kept slipping in their blood and their screaming filled my ears until I woke up sobbing. I was lucky that Mam had already gone out to start the chores.

5.

The next day I made my own count of the cartridges, and whatever else we could use to protect ourselves: knives, cast-iron pots, shovels and loys and Da's two big sickles. Mam killed another chicken and bled it out. It was a waste, but if she knew what I had done with the devil it would be the whip for me. She had it out now, coiled on the ground by her feet as she wrung out the chicken.

Beside it lay the revolver. I wasn't sure what that meant, but I didn't like it.

"Addy," she called.

I went over and reached for the chicken, but she handed me the revolver, then the bowl of blood.

"I need your help," she said. "We don't have time

for her games and I can't have her sicking up again."
She took up the whip and gave it a good crack. When
it struck the ground it made places on my body hurt.
"Keep the gun behind your back so she can't see it.
That's it. Now when we go in there, you just get that
blood down her throat. I'll do the rest. If she breaks
loose, shoot her dead."

She waited until I nodded, then led the way to the
barn, her skirts tossing the dust one way and another.
As we swung the door open, a buzzard rose off the
horse at the noise and Mam threw a rock at it with a
cry. I hated when she was like this, raging and
stamping her feet and with her shoulders pulled up.
Before Da died she never got angry. She had been
kind and gentle, always laughing and singing. She was
still kind sometimes, but more and more she was this
Mam, almost like she wanted to be angry. *I'm doing this
for you*, she always told me. *I'm doing this so you won't be
afraid of anything. Fear is death out here, Addy. Never forget
that.*

We went to the stall and I was afraid the devil
would give us away, but she only looked from Mam to
me and back again. Mam held up the whip and she
flinched.

"You need to eat," Mam said in a loud voice.
"Now you're going to drink this and you're going to
like it, understand?"

"I'm doing my best," the devil said. "There are
other kinds of blood that suit me better, as well you
know."

"Don't give me that. Blood is blood." Mam nodded at me. "Addy, help her drink."

"Like meat is meat?" The devil's eyebrows raised. "I don't see you two dining on rats, or that horseflesh rotting out there. No, it's all chickens and sweet little goats for you."

I stopped halfway towards her, swallowing. Mam uncoiled the whip. "Addy, give her the bowl."

As I got close the devil looked up at me and mouthed *bargain*, and then she took a sip from the bowl. She gagged at once, pushing me away as she strained to work it down, just as I had struggled to swallow the stew Mam made out of Isaac. Her face became damp and she made a choking noise.

"More," Mam said. "She needs to drink it all."

I started to angle the bowl and the devil shook her head. "Wait," she gasped. "Wait, I—" She broke off, gagging.

"For God's sake," Mam yelled. She cracked the whip and I cried out as it whistled past me and struck the devil in the face. "Addy, get it down her throat!"

But I couldn't move for looking. The whip had opened a cut on the devil's face, a big ugly gash that was running dark blood. Only as I watched, the blood became sticky and the edges puffed up, then moved together. At first I thought my eyes were playing tricks, I blinked and blinked, but every time I blinked the cut looked better. As if it was healing right in front of me.

"Mam, what's she doing?" I whispered.

"I told you, Addy," she said, and there was something heavy in her voice. "She's a child of the serpent, a devil made flesh. You can't kill 'em like you would a man. Right now, the only things keeping her from killing us are the blade in her backside and her hunger." She pointed with the whip. "Now get that god-damned chicken blood down her throat."

"A devil made flesh," the devil repeated. "You should try looking in the mirror. Singing hymns while you whip me? Plotting murders? I think you *want* this. I think you're *enjoying* yourself. I think you like the whip and you like blood and you even like killing. I think you even like it when your girl misbehaves, you like getting her scared and making her bleed, I bet you tell her it's for her own good—"

The whip came crashing down, over and over, lashing one way and another. I stepped out of the stall, hugging the bowl to myself and my eyes shut tight, trying not to hear the devil screaming and Mam humming under her breath.

Then all of a sudden there was silence, just the sounds of panting, and Mam said, "Addy, give her the bowl again."

I opened my eyes and the devil looked like she was in pieces, her clothes hanging in ribbons and her face all red gashes. She had one eye swelling and her mouth hung open. I could see her heaving.

"Addy," Mam said in a soft voice, "give our guest something to drink, or I'll turn her blood to dust."

Slowly I walked towards the devil. I saw now she was crying, her tears mixing with her blood, and I felt like crying too. "She means it," I said, forcing the words out. "She knows how."

"All she knows," the devil muttered, "is cruelty."

"Please," I whispered.

She looked up at me, her good eye black and red and swimming in tears, but she opened her mouth and drank the chicken blood down, throatful after throatful.

And then she jerked away, wrenching in the yoke as she began choking. Mam ran behind her and seized her jaw, holding her mouth closed. "Get the revolver out," she said to me. I pulled it out of my pants and held it with both hands, keeping it pointed steady at the devil's face. Her cheeks puffed out and her swollen eye cracked open; she was gagging and mewling as Mam kept her mouth shut tight.

And I remembered, suddenly: when Da had died, I was sick soon after, and Mam had given me some medicine, something foul. It was a medicine I'd had before, only it tasted like it had gone sour, but when I tried to tell her how bad it tasted she had flown into a rage. She had poured it into my mouth, more than I'd ever taken, and then held my mouth shut, and I had sicked up inside so much I nearly choked. Later she had said how sorry she was, that grief was making her act strange.

"She'll shoot you," Mam was saying. "She'll shoot you dead unless you keep that god-damned blood down." The devil was going still at last, though she looked worse than I'd ever seen her. She looked like she might even die.

"Good girl," Mam said. Slowly she released her hands. "Good girl." She stepped back and the devil sagged limp. "See?" She pushed the devil's hair out of her face, then gave her a pat on the head. "Now that wasn't so bad, was it? No more games, now. You just drink, and you kill Bill Boyland, and everything will be just fine." She wiped her hands on her skirts. "Come on, Addy. We got work to do."

Grief, Mam had said. But that had all been years ago. What was she grieving now? Or did she still miss Da that much?

"You'll pay for this." The devil's voice was raspy. "You just wait. You think you know things? Everything you know is nothing more than the fancies of sick old men. And we took care of them a long time ago."

Mam picked up the bowl and handed it to me, then settled about coiling the whip up neat. She'd started humming.

"But I know something." The devil's voice rose until it filled the barn. "I know you're a fucking *liar*. I know this has nothing to do with the land because it was *never yours*. You're using me to mete out some kind of vengeance. You pretend you're just a poor old woman done wrong by, but at the end of the day you're nothing but a pisspoor squatter and when they come, they'll hang you and good riddance!"

I reached for Mam who had turned back, but she only looked at the devil, then at me with a broad smile, and I realized she was trying not to laugh.

"Seems like chicken blood agrees with her after all." And with a chuckle she strode out of the barn, singing,

A noble army, men and boys,
the matron and the maid,
around the Savior's throne rejoice,
in robes of light arrayed.
They climbed the steep ascent of heaven,
through peril, toil and pain;
O God, to us may grace be given,
to follow in their train.

When we were getting ready for bed Mam suddenly said, "You want to ask me a question, Addy, ask me. You know you can ask me anything."

I slowly buttoned up my nightshirt. I could just glimpse my reflection in Mam's little mirror, that she had brought with her when we came out. It was the only fancy thing we had, with a frame made up of tiny flowers and ribbons all tangling together. *From my old life*, she would say when I asked her about it. *It reminds me that we're all a mix of good and bad, like your Da says. And that God wants us to live with our decisions.*

I looked at myself, at my short hair and my peaky face. I was a mix of things, all right. I'd never even seen a girl like me, and I sure didn't know what was good or bad right now. But there were things being decided that I was going to have to live with.

"What if we asked Bill Boyland to buy us out," I said, choosing my words carefully. "We could go somewhere else and start over, maybe somewhere closer to the railroad."

I tensed then, waiting for her to start yelling, maybe even to hit me. But she only sighed. "Addy, you can't get caught up in wanting to change things. Change is never as good as it looks in your head. There're always problems, there're always men looking to take whatever you have—your money, your land, your pride. At some point, even a woman has to take a stand, or you'll always be running."

She laid down and closed her eyes, but I blurted out, "Is that why you and Da came here, because you were running?"

Mam opened her eyes and looked at me for a long moment. But all she said was, "Running means different things to men and women." She rolled over, turning her back to me.

"I don't understand," I said.

But she didn't say anything, she only lay there. I knew she was awake and holding herself tight and still, like she had after Da died. All day crying and laughing over him in the field while I had walked the long, long road to Tom's place, and then when they took Da away she had laid down just like this. Only Da was seven years gone now, and I was still alive.

Later that night I left the house again. I had my dirty rags, but I also took a clean one. Outside I found the bowl and the skinning knife and brought everything into the shadow of the barn. There I hesitated, looking at the big cruel knife, but there was nothing for it, and it felt right that it should be this way. I had done Isaac wrong; I had done them all wrong, all these years, telling them they were going off to Tom's to eat grass. Now I thought maybe I had known otherwise but I had wanted to believe it. The stew Mam made had tasted horrible, but it had also tasted familiar.

I cut my left hand at the base of my thumb. I didn't use that hand so much, and I made the cut low so it wouldn't rub against the plow. At first it didn't hurt but then it did, oh God did it hurt, and it was hard not to bandage it at once but let the blood run into the bowl. So much pain. How long had Isaac suffered for, before God took him? What about all the others, the chickens and the little ox and the devil's horse and even Da, what had they felt?

As if I was speaking out loud, something moved out by the horse, something that was picking at whatever scraps were left on the bones made blue by the starlight. There was no moon, I realized, not even the sliver anymore.

All sorts of things can happen in the dark.

When I started to feel faint, I pressed the cut closed and tied it with the clean rag, and then I took everything into the barn.

The devil was hunched over in the yoke. The whole stall smelled of sick; she was surrounded by puddles of the stuff, all sticky and shiny. When I stepped inside she flinched and tried to move away.

"Bargain," I whispered. I held out the rags and the bowl.

She angled her head at me, as if trying to read something on my face. Her eye was open again but only just, and though her cuts had closed up I could see them still, pale lines that ran all over her.

"Bowl first," she finally said.

I brought it close to her open mouth and tilted it, just letting the blood dribble in. She drank like she was thirsty. Her cold hand touched mine, bringing the bowl closer, and she drank it all, making me turn it until she got every drop out. I started to take the bowl away, but her hand grabbed mine hard and kept the bowl close while she licked it clean with long strokes of her tongue, like a cat. When at last she let me go, there were smears of blood on her face. She tried to rub them off with her bound hands and then lick them.

The lines on her face and body were gone.

I gave her the rags and she began sucking. She looked almost healthy, like she had fattened up just from that little bit of blood.

"I'm sorry," I said.

She was silent, sucking on the cloth.

"It's just—things have been hard since Da died."

Still she sucked on the cloth. I was trying to think of what to say next when she abruptly spat it out and said, "I have not been beaten like that since I was a child." Her voice sounded different, low and full. "I swore I would *never* be beaten like that again."

"The serpent beat you?" I frowned, trying to imagine it.

At that she laughed, so loud I hushed her. "I have

parents, Addy, just like you. A mother. A father who passed. It was my aunt who did the beating in my family, for as long as we let her." Slowly her tongue ran over her lips. "I don't let her anymore."

"You have a family?"

"Of course I have a family. I also have friends, a lover, and a *name*. I even owned a horse once." At the last her voice went soft.

I didn't know what to say. She went back to suckling and I crouched down, rocking on my heels. All of a sudden I could see her people, a whole lot of people who looked like her, who might be missing her. Maybe they just healed fast because they were lucky, maybe the scales on her neck were just a rash, or a birthmark, like the boy in town who had a big red patch on his face.

"This all feels *bad*." Her voice was so quiet, I wasn't sure if she was speaking to me. "It feels like more than just a land dispute; it feels like an old grudge, maybe even from before your Da." She gave the rag a lick. "Times are changing, Addy. You can't just go about killing a man, not anymore. The Bill Boylands can still bend the law because they have money and men, but even that's coming to an end. There are laws now, laws and officers to enforce them. More's the pity," she added, smiling a little.

"Mam says a woman has to take a stand," I said.

"A stand for what? For a scrap of land? For something that happened years ago?" She shook her head. "The past is gone, Addy. The only thing worth taking a stand for is the future, the best possible future for those you love. Take it from someone who has an awful lot of past behind her."

I frowned. "Maybe it shouldn't be one or the other, though. Maybe it should be about balancing them, like everything is supposed to be balanced."

"Oh yes, I forgot, your father and his bloody balance." She laughed softly. "God save us from—"

But she stopped short. Her head turned in the yoke, straining the ropes. "They're coming," she whispered.

"Who's coming?"

"At least eight horses—? And some kind of cart, or a wagon." She looked at me, her eyes black again. "Take the blade out."

I stood up, uneasy. "I don't think ..." But then I heard it too. Faint, like the first hint of a storm coming. It made everything go cold, even the pain in my hand. My mind seemed to empty all at once, I couldn't think on what to do.

There was a cracking noise, and suddenly a hand seized mine, icy and so strong. She had pulled free of the stall and her hand was free. And then the rag was gone and she was sucking at the cut, biting it and sucking, and I screamed then because nothing had hurt like this before. She was chewing me up and I couldn't get free, she seemed made of stone. I flailed and pulled and my free hand set upon a fork and I swung it at her. She fell to her side but it didn't seem to even hurt her. She just began working the yoke off.

"Take it out," she gasped. "Addy, take the fucking blade out!"

I barely heard her. I was pressing my hand tight, too scared to even look at it, it felt so raw. Her lips were shiny with my blood. *You'll take our throats*, Mam had said.

"Addy!" She was hanging off the ropes, trying to stay upright. "Addy, listen to me. I promise you I won't let anything happen to you. I give you my word. I can stop them, I can stop them all, but you have to take the blade out. For the love of your Mam and your goats and everything you hold dear, *take the blade out*."

I didn't know what to do. Everything seemed to be happening at once. I could hear the horses and a few shouts now and Mam calling my name and the animals were bleating and squawking and I could still smell the dead horse and what was I supposed to do?

"Addy, *please*."

I tried, then. I tried to see her as Mam saw her, like a rabid dog to sic on people. But all I could see was how her hands were trembling, and Isaac's little feet, and the way the horse had to be dragged like it knew what was coming. Whatever this all was, it wasn't balance, much less anything good or right.

I got behind her and seized the handle and pulled as hard as I could, but she shrieked and waved her hand.

"No," she gasped. "Open it, you have to open it."

I felt the handle until I found the bump and pressed it. She wailed behind gritted teeth and then I pulled while she gasped, "harder, harder," and I put my foot on her back and rocked it back and forth like

a stuck spade until it suddenly came free in a spray of
blood.

With a cry I flung the knife aside and started to
run for the door but she seized my ankle and I fell.
She pulled me back as I screamed and hollered for
Mam, then grabbed my chin and pulled my head
against her chest.

"Forgive me," she whispered.

And then she bit my neck, and the pain flared
sharp and stabbing and then everything went soft,
soft, like a blanket had been dropped over me. All soft.
It seemed only a minute—or maybe it was hours—
when she finally let me go and I dropped onto the
ground. I watched as her boot stepped over me, only
to twist and stumble. She fell on top of me and I felt
her weight but no pain, no pain. She got to her knees
and began crawling towards the barn door. Just before
the doorway, she pulled herself up using the post and
carefully unhooked one of the sickles. She stood for a
moment, wobbling like a newborn kid; and then she
kicked the door open and fell forward into the night.

6.

Everything was foggy, though it wasn't the time for
fog. My hand was throbbing sore and my neck ached.
I got to my feet but I couldn't see the barn doors; and
then I saw them, only they kept swaying. I managed
to walk to them by looking through them, at the space
between them, which was glowing with a bright
orange light.

I stepped out into a world on fire. Everywhere was shimmering with heat and flame, the smoke covered the stars. There was screaming, close and far off all at once, from everywhere and nowhere. I looked behind me and the barn was licked with flame, the hills sparking red.

It was hell. We had called the devil down and I had let her loose and she had brought us all to hell.

I made my heavy legs walk. The smoke caught in my throat, setting me to coughing. The goat pen stood open and empty. There were shapes in the far corner, small and still. I looked at them and I knew they were gone, yet I kept hearing them bleating like Isaac had bleated, all mixed up with the shouts and screams of the men and the echoing gunshots and a woman crying or laughing or both—

Mam.

There was no more house. There was only fire, curling around the beams and the chimney Da had laid stone by stone. I opened my mouth to call to Mam but started coughing. A hand caught me by the arm and spun me around. Before me stood a man, sooty and wild-eyed. He shook me hard over and over.

"I got the kid!" he hollered.

My head was snapping against my neck. My teeth flew up and bit my tongue hard. Blood filled my mouth. He swung me one way and another, peering into the smoke and flame.

"Bill!" he hollered again. "Bill, I got the kid! Bill—"

Something bright shot across his throat and it opened up and was full of blood. My mouth was full of blood. He tried to speak and instead he fell over, his hand still gripping my arm, his tongue sticking out like Isaac's. I started screaming then, I screamed as I never had before. The devil swung the sickle up and down into his chest. She was covered in blood. Blood sprayed out of the man as she wrenched the sickle up and brought it down again. Cold air ran over my belly and I looked down at the red cut in my nightshirt. Someone was screaming and screaming, and it was me, I was turning inside out with screaming. I tore more at my shirt but I wasn't cut, the sickle had only caught the fabric.

"Addy." The devil's voice was huge and echoing in the night. She bent and reached into the blood, her hand disappeared in the blood, and when she pulled it out with a grunt there was something round and wet in her palm. She held it out to me. "See? That's all a man is inside. No evil, no divinity, not even your god-damn balance. Just flesh. That's why your Da and his people failed: because they could never bring them-selves to believe this. This is all there is."

Seizing my cut hand, she pressed the organ into it, still warm, and my voice broke then from screaming. I dropped it and covered my eyes, waiting to feel her hands on me. But there was nothing. I peeked through my fingers, then lowered my hands.

The devil was gone.

The man at my feet looked different. With his kerchief twisted I could see how frightened he was and how young, as young as me. Everywhere now I saw the bodies of men: men in pieces, men with heads staved in and throats cut, men sprawled and men lying so peaceful they might have been asleep.

There was no more howling now, but I heard the crying laughter again and walked towards it.

The yard was another world. Everything was gusting smoke. I wiped my face and my hand came away smeared with blood and ash. The cut on my hand throbbed and my neck too. Somewhere far away a man screamed and began pleading, and I turned one way and another but the wind carried him away. Only the crying laughter seemed fixed.

Soon I came upon a trail in the dirt and followed it to the beech tree. It seemed like I had walked for miles, but when I looked around there were the ruins of the house and barn, as close as they had always been.

Under the beech tree was a body and Mam was standing over him, her skirts hiked up and her foot on his face. I saw Bill Boyland's fancy gold watch hanging from his clothes. Her face screwed up and her leg flexed as she pressed down. She was giggling and weeping all at once.

As I drew close, something cracked, and her foot sank lower.

She looked at me and then back at the man. Her face was wet. "I never knew," she said. "Look at how soft a man is. I never knew."

Beneath her foot all was red and black. She took her foot away and laughed again, that strange, weeping laugh, and it was that morning with Da all over again.

"Look, Addy." She nudged at his face with the toe of her shoe and Bill Boyland's eyeball pushed forward. I shrieked and she laughed. "An eye for an eye, how do you like that? An eye for an eye. Sometimes God does answer our prayers."

"Mam," I said. I could barely speak for trembling. "Mam, we have to do something."

"You let her out, Adelaide Norton," she said. "You disobeyed me and you went to her and you let her out."

"Mam," I said again. "Mam, we need to …" But I couldn't think of what we needed to do. I kept looking at where Bill Boyland's face had been, at that one shiny eyeball.

"I had a plan," Mam said. "I was going to tell them I had a woman in my barn, I was going to offer her to Bill Boyland as a payoff, to spare you and I. He would go in to have her and she would kill him." She pointed at my neck. "Now you got her taint on you, and there ain't no fixing that."

"She couldn't drink that other blood!" My heart was pounding. "She couldn't drink it and you knew it! She would have died if I hadn't—" I broke off then, because suddenly the thought filled my head and it was awful. "Or did you know I was going out there to her?"

Mam just looked at me. The fist filled my throat, pressing down so much I felt sick. I opened my mouth but nothing would come out, not words or tears. Slow and careful, Mam reached into her skirt pocket and pulled out the revolver and aimed it at me. The barrel was so large. It was as large as a scream, as large as the hole we had buried Da in.

She stepped over Bill Boyland's legs and I closed my eyes, but nothing happened. When I opened them again the barrel was pointing just past my ear, and I turned and looked over my shoulder.

The devil stood there, Mam's whip in her hand. Her eyes were black. Two long pointed teeth filled her mouth, stained dark against the white bone.

"You're not tainted, Addy," she said in her strange, huge voice. "But you need to walk away now. Your Mam and I have unfinished business."

"No!" I looked from one to the other. "Please. You can go now, we said you could go when you stopped them. Can't she, Mam?"

Mam said nothing, only cocked the trigger.

"I made a promise to myself a long time ago." The devil was staring at Mam. "And a woman is nothing without her word."

"Amen," Mam said. "And now we see you for what you really are."

The devil pointed at Bill Boyland. "Amen."

It happened all at once, then. Mam shoved me and fired and the whip snaked out, catching Mam's wrist and sending the revolver flying into the air. We all three cried out and fell to the ground. The shot echoed against the hills.

Mam's wrist was bleeding. She began crawling in

the dirt, looking for the revolver. "Find the gun," she whispered. "Hurry, Addy."

The devil was on her hands and knees, hunched over, her sides heaving, and then she staggered to her feet.

"Please," I said.

"Addy, find the god-damned gun!" Mam cried.

"Please just go," I said.

The devil looked at me with those black, flat eyes. She pressed her fingers into her chest, all the way inside. With a grimace she twisted and dug and when she held up her hand again it was glistening black. Blood dripped off the fingers that held up Mam's bullet like it was something precious.

She flicked it at Mam. It sailed through the air and struck Mam in the face.

"Shitty poison by shitty alchemists," she said, but her voice was thick like she was sick again.

"It'll burn you up," Mam said. She was shaking; I had never seen Mam shake before. "You're done for, serpent! You're going back to hell where you came from!"

"My name is Elisabeth," the devil said, "and the only hells are the ones we make."

The whip rose up, catching smoke as it shot curling into the sky. When it came down Mam hunched over, covering her head with her hands.

"Stop it!" I got to my feet; it was then that I saw the revolver at the base of the beech tree.

Again the whip cracked. I ran as fast I could and seized the revolver. My hands were shaking as I swung it around. She was almost on top of Mam, swinging the whip up and down.

Not once did Mam cry out.

"Stop it or I'll shoot!" I yelled.

The devil went still, looking at me, the whip dangling from her hand.

"Shoot her," Mam hissed. "Shoot her dead."

I steadied the revolver, sighting the devil square in the face. "Go away," I said loudly. "Just go. You did what we asked, now we're keeping our promise."

"For the love of God, Addy, shoot the bitch!"

I glanced at Mam. Her mouth was hanging funny; the whip had caught her in the face. I turned back to the devil who hadn't moved, who just looked at me with the same steady gaze. I curled my finger around the trigger.

"Elisabeth," I said. "Please, please just go."

"God-damn it!" Mam yelled. "What's wrong with you? She's just an animal, put her down!"

There was a shot, and a second and a third, though I hadn't done anything. I looked at the revolver and suddenly the devil was spinning me around and holding my hands and together we squeezed. The man behind us bucked and fell. The devil pointed again, squeezing my finger a second time, so hard I thought it would break. His body jumped and went still.

I looked over at Mam and she was facedown in the dirt and I knew she was dead. I knew she was dead. All the air left the world. I reached for her only my hand was all cut up still, I would taint her with my touch. Everything seemed wrong. I looked at Mam's wet hair and I looked at the cuts on my hand. I knew. I knew.

Liquid splashed on the ground. It took all my strength to turn away from Mam and look at her. The devil had a flask and she was pouring water on where Mam had shot her. My arm rose up and I aimed the revolver at her head.

The devil went still. "Addy," she said, "your mother was a cruel, frightened woman—"

"I told you to leave." My voice sounded different, deeper than I had ever heard it before, almost like I was the devil now.

Slowly she raised her hands. "There will be more coming, by daybreak if not sooner. We need to strip the bodies, make it look like a robbery—"

"Go away," I said in the same dark voice. "Go away and don't ever come back, or I swear to God I'll kill you."

And I meant it. I meant every word. She looked so small from behind the revolver. How was it that we had feared her? It would be nothing to shoot her or cut her with the sickles. Nothing to watch her bleed out like a spilled jug.

My insides ached so bad I wished I was dead.

Slowly the devil took a step backwards, and then another, keeping her hands up. She looked so small. It would be nothing to squeeze the trigger, nothing to watch her flinch and cry out and fall; nothing and everything. I dropped to my knees, the revolver huge and heavy in my hands, breaking my fingers from its awful weight. All around me was the smoke and the dead and I was as good as. It was nothing to kill a person and it was everything. All of it cruel, the gun and the knife and the whip; all of it a flat blackness like the devil's eyes and Mam's too, when she had stepped on Bill Boyland's face. All of it as flat as Isaac's eyes when the life went from him.

I looked at Mam and I knew she was dead. I crawled to her and laid my good hand on her, the untainted one, and turned her on her side so she would be comfortable. I wanted to cry but the fist was solid inside me. Instead I smoothed back her hair and closed her eyes and mouth; I put her hands together so she could pray, wherever she had gone to. I thought to sing then, like she would sing to me when I was little, but no words would come. Instead I sat by her in silence while the world burned to the ground.

7.

It was the sun that made me move. That first gleam of light made everything visible. I saw every body stark against the ground, saw the house and the barn like they were more real now for being ruined. Smoke rose up into the sky, high enough that it could be easily seen from town.

I hurried then. I wanted more than anything to bury Mam but I couldn't. I kissed her forehead one last time. She would have been proud of me: I hadn't cried, not once, I had just sat there swallowing it all back and pushing it down until I didn't even feel the fist anymore, until I didn't feel anything at all. How many nights had Mam done the same after Da died? Pressing it down until she was empty, waking up to the same hard dirt in the fields.

In the cold blue dawn it seemed a terrible thing that Da had done, bringing us here.

I took the pants and shirt off one of the least dirty bodies, and the coat off another. I dressed as quick as I could, then ripped my nightshirt and threw it in the brush. Maybe they would think I got carried off.

The goat pen and chicken coop were ashes. I started trembling at the sight but I pushed it away until I was empty again. Instead I set about digging through the men's pockets, taking whatever was worth something: money, watches, even their spare cartridges. What I couldn't fit in my pockets I bundled in kerchiefs and tied to my belt.

The only horse left was the mare tied to the cart— not even a wagon, just a small cart with its wheel stuck against a tree. I came up on the cart slow. I didn't want to spook her; she still looked wild-eyed. Only as I held out my hand I heard not a whinny but a bleating, and something moved in the shadows under the cart, and then all of a sudden little Addy stood there, sooty but bleating and bleating and I was hugging her close, smelling her good smell and her licking both my hands clean. And there was Rachel and a little one I hadn't named, he had been born just fine and never needed naming, but now his fur was matted with blood and he hung back until I called, "Joseph, Joseph," and he came to me and it was everything. I understood, then, that this was what was meant by grace, how in the midst of so much wrong there could be something that was beautiful and right.

I cleaned out the unlit torches and the corked jugs of beer from the cart and got the goats up inside. They seemed happy to be leaving. I searched the brush, but I couldn't find any of the others, and then it was time. It took the horse a little while to trust me, but I coaxed her back and forward again and she understood and that was a kind of grace too. There was a whip in its socket and I threw that away with the rest. When I saw little Addy watching me I told her, "No more," and I meant it. No more of such things, ever. Together the horse and I steered the cart onto the road, and with every step I said "thank you" and I meant that too. I had never felt so grateful.

Once I was up in the seat, though, I found myself trembling again. From there the ruin of our land seemed a sorry thing, small and empty. Even Mam's body seemed little more than a spot against the dirt. I stopped the horse so I could really look at it all, one last time. There was something white and crumpled beside her: my nightshirt had blown up against her, so it looked there was an Addy curled up next to her. So I was up on the road, alone, and down there was an Addy who had stayed by Mam to the end.

I touched my face and my cheeks were all wet, though it didn't feel like I was crying, I wasn't crying at all. Perhaps the other Addy got to cry at the end, perhaps Mam had let her, just the once.

The horse began walking without me telling her

to and I let her have her head. I felt a little better for moving. The hills were warming into their browns and greens, and all the clouds were white against the blue sky. It was almost right, save for the aching inside me, save for how sore my throat was from holding everything in. It had all been wrong from the start, it had started wrong and ended worse. Little Addy came up and nudged my elbow and I began laughing even though I was still crying, and I understood better how Mam must have felt all tumbled up inside. Maybe she had known it was wrong, only there was nothing for it but to see it through. *A woman has to take a stand*, but it was worthless if you weren't standing for something right.

Behind me Joseph butted Rachel and she gave him a nip and little Addy wiggled onto the seat beside me, standing tall and proud. It reminded me of when we first came out here: we had passed by some folks camped by a river and they had been singing. The sun had lit up the water and the grass had been green as far as the eye could see and Da had said, *We're gonna make this God's garden, Addy,* and the people had sung so prettily, nothing like my trembling voice now:

> *There let my way appear*
> *Steps unto heaven*
> *All that Thou sendest me*
> *In mercy given*
> *Angels to beckon me*
> *Nearer, my God, to Thee*
> *Nearer to Thee*

I sang and little Addy bleated and I was sad but I was alive, I was alive, the fist loosening and my heart aching. I was alive and I had to stay alive, for now I had promises to keep, and a grace I dared not squander.

OTHER BOOKS BY L.S. JOHNSON

Vacui Magia: Stories

Harkworth Hall

Leviathan

To stay up-to-date on new stories, works in progress, and exclusive offers like ARCs, sign up for her newsletter at www.traversingz.com.

ACKNOWLEDGMENTS

It takes a village, always. This book would not have been possible without the generous encouragement of fellow writers, editors, and readers, who encouraged my work over the years and made me do better each and every time. Special thanks are due to Rhonda Parrish, who was a graceful shepherd for no less than three stories in this volume; Kat Howard for her always-brilliant editing; Rose Fox and Daniel José Older, for that first amazing acceptance all those years ago; and Sian Jones, for being the best cheerleader, critter, and wingwoman all in one package - I am lucky to call you friend. Charlotte Ashley, as always, tried to impose order on my grammatical chaos, and George Cotronis designed the cover with his own particular eye for the beauty in darkness. And last but not least, never least, thank *you*, reader: for reading, for responding, for being on the other end of the line.

STORY NOTES AND CONTENT WARNINGS

Rare Birds, 1959

Content warning for sexual violence. First published in *C Is for Chimera*, Poise and Pen Publishing, 2016. "Rare Birds, 1959" has been revised for this publication.

Marigolds

First published in *Long Hidden: Speculative Fiction from the Margins of History*, Crossed Genres Publications, 2014.

Properties of Obligate Pearls

First published in *New Haven Review*, Issue 020, Summer 2017.

Sabbaths

First published in *Syntax & Salt*, Issue 1, March 2018.

The Queen of Lakes

First published in *Fae*, World Weaver Press, 2014.

We Are Sirens

First published in *Sirens*, World Weaver Press, 2016. "We Are Sirens" has been revised for this publication.

A Harvest Fit for Monsters

First published in *Nightscript IV*, 2018.

To Us May Grace Be Given

Content warning for violence to animals. First published in *GigaNotoSaurus*, October 2017.

CPSIA information can be obtained
at www.ICGtesting.com
Printed in the USA
LVHW051007030220
645650LV00002B/379